I r o n Bridge Sunday

and

Other Stories

Les M. Brown

REDHAWK
PUBLICATIONS

Redhawk Publications
The Catawba Valley Community College Press
2550 US Hwy 70 SE
Hickory NC 28602

ISBN: 978-1-959346-22-7

Library of Congress Number: 2023946456

Layout and edit by Robert Canipe and Tim Peeler

Printed in the United States of America

redhawkpublications.com

This is a work of fiction. Any similarities to persons living or dead, or actual events is purely coincidental.

Advance praise for *Iron Bridge Sunday and Other Stories...*

Iron Bridge Sunday is the most beautiful collection of pitch perfect short stories that I have ever encountered---each one encompassing a whole existence. These hard lives are held together by love, cruelty, necessity, family lore and custom and hard work...and Les Brown writes the best dialogue I've ever read, hands down. I hope *Iron Bridge Sunday* will find the wide readership it deserves.

—Lee Smith, author of *Saving Grace* and *News of the Spirit*

Iron Bridge Sunday is a wonderful book. Brown is a master of regional dialect, and his humor is laugh out loud funny as his characters wend their way through their lives, but there is also a poignancy, and as we read the last powerful line, we feel the heartache of a place and people lost to time. Les Brown is one of our Appalachia's most gifted storytellers.

—Ron Rash, author of *The Caretaker* and *Serena*

Much has been made about the importance of place in southern American fiction. Les Brown's *Iron Bridge Sunday and Other Stories* masterfully weaves the tales of two generations of farm and otherwise rural families, and in doing so, creates the fictional Sycamore Cove, an unforgettable space that is charged with natural beauty and gifted with a landscape that is a challenge for humans to conquer. The setting is so true; one gets the feeling that these delightful stories could not have taken place anywhere else.

—Tim Peeler, author of *Knucklebear* and *Rough Beast*

Les Brown's *Iron Bridge Sunday and Other Stories* couldn't be more engaging. A portrait of life in a Western North Carolina mountain cove in the previous century, the stories are funny, sad, harsh, even violent. Taken as a whole, they add up to a complex rendering of a hardscrabble time when people were more connected to the land and to each other. It's an evocation of a way of life mostly gone, written by someone who lived the life himself. In its sensibility, its empathy, its humor and its hard-earned tenderness, Iron Bridge Sunday and Other Stories is reminiscent of Fred Chappell's classic *I Am One of You Forever*.

—Tommy Hays, author of *The Pleasure Was Mine* and *What I Came to Tell You*

Also by Les M. Brown:

The Place Where Trees Had Names, Poems, 2020

Cold Forge, Poems, 2022

Dedication

For my wife and patient reviewer of the text, Joyce Compton Brown, and for Tom Rash, Anne Kaylor and Leslie Rupracht for their editing skills as well as for Tommy Hayes for his invaluable encouragement.

Publications and Acknowledgements

The author thanks the editors of the following publications in whose journals these stories first appeared.

Appalachian Heritage: "Loops and Fireworks"
Broad River Review: "Iron Bridge Sunday"
County Lines: "Silvertone"
Moonshine Review: "The Sheriff Thwarts a Robbery at Homer Waycaster's Store," (Published under the title, "Black and White")
Now and Then: "The Cage"
Potato Soup Journal: "Love Path"

The author thanks the following organizations and their judges for recognition given to the stories listed below.

Western North Carolina Writers Network: "Bastard"
Elizabeth Simpson Short Story Contest: 3rd place, "The Poker Game"
MHLF 3rd place, James Still Prize for Short Story: "Jehue and the Hamond Organ"
MHLF 3rd place, Jesse Stuart Prize for Young Adults: "The Flats"
Franklin County Arts, Carolina Writing Contest, Honorable Mention: "Silvertone"

Contents

Part III Billy in the Blue Ridge

Prologue

He was one of the boys who grew up in Sycamore Cove, carrying generations of stories told by fathers, uncles and aunts, the boys who lived in this Appalachian valley, testing its limits and their own, pushing life's boundaries with innocent abandon. He is the product of oral history, of a community of vital youth, a small country school, a family of love, of firebrand preachers, of denial, and sad destiny. He is as much a product of that valley as the grain, the cattle, and the forest it grew. He has flowed like the water of Laurel Creek through the valley beyond its boundaries, but he is destined to return as the rain returns the water to flow again. His name is Billy Fletcher.

Billy's world was a place where men in overalls, aproned women, and their children held forth in lives of unity. Some were protected by youth and work and God in a fertile land of clear flowing water and deep cool woods rich with hemlock and laurel. Some would fly from the valley to search beyond the mountains, to test a world spoken of in a small school where all were as one. Others would stay to lose their innocence or deny anything beyond their mountain-bound contentment. These memories, images, and people defined Billy's childhood.

Part I

Ancestral Shenanigans

Questions of Sobriety, Celebrations, Natural Disasters, and Peculiar Plantings

B illy's life was shaped by legends, tall tales, and the sometimes crude and the raucous humor of his ancestors. Those stories of shenanigans were as much a part of his heritage as the land he would eventually receive from his father. Sunday afternoons, Christmas celebrations, any holiday that involved the gathering of the clan, gradually drifted from talks of present-day woes and pleasures to stories of grandfathers, great uncles, their wives, and ancestors long gone but never allowed to rest in peace. Billy understood his grandfather, Elihue, more from the family stories than from that vague figure of an old man reading Zane Grey novels in his isolated room with a bottle perhaps quietly tucked under a nearby quilt. Billy knew the stories and told them long after the original tellers had moved to their own legendary status and added a second generation of tales.

Elihue and his two brothers, Clifford and Martin, who lived nearby, were the first generation of descendants from the original settlers of Sycamore Cove. The fields and pastures between Bobcat and Buckeye mountains had provided a good living for the Fletchers. Two of the large, austere white houses, built for function and not show, were in hollering distance of each other. And often hollering was the simplest way for Elihue and Clifford to communicate. Martin lived farther down Sycamore Cove on his part of the divided farm. For some time he farmed and operated a roller mill on Laurel Creek just downstream from Elihue. None of them was known for temperance. Their father, Daniel, had operated a licensed still on the cold, clear Wildcat Branch that ran down a cliff-bound steep hollow on Buckeye Mountain.

They were all bald as peeled onions except for little fringes that grew no higher than their ears. The three of them had about as much respect for civility as feral cats, and the valley echoed with their antics. One day Elihue and Clifford were standing out in a field of young corn, talking over farm matters when they heard Martin hollering at them a quarter of a mile away. "Hey, Elihue."

Clifford, sizing up the situation, figured that Martin was drunk. "Just don't pay him any attention, Elihue, he's lit."

Again, Martin repeated the call, "Heyyy Elihue!" They ignored him.

"Heyyy Elihue!" echoed again and again.

Finally, Elihue, deciding that something must be wrong, yelled at the top of his lungs, "Whatcha want, Martin?" True to Clifford's suspicion, Martin yelled back as loud as he could, "Go to Hell, Elihue!"

Clifford and Elihue liked to camp. It was an excuse to get away from their wives, strong women who ruled their household domains. Elihue's wife, Lillian, was firm, but Hannah, Clifford's wiry, stern wife, habitually laid into him about tracking mud into the house and spitting tobacco juice between his fingers onto the front steps where company would see it, or worse, step in it.

On one occasion the men drank, lied, laughed and talked until they had to crawl to their old makeshift canvas tent. As they slept in their nocturnal stupor in the meadow beside a spring near Laurel Creek, the campfire embers died at some point, and organic anesthesia caused bodily functions to relax and release. Clifford crawled out of the tent on the dew-soaked grass, dragging himself upright at the edge of the camp site. His long johns drooped as he relieved himself. Elihue roused enough to hear Clifford say, "It's clear as a bell, cold as Hell and everthing smells like crap."

One spring afternoon Clifford and Elihue acquired a jug full of moonshine from a local bootlegger. The two brothers disappeared into the woods beyond a field of young corn recently hilled up and hoed out. Hours passed. Lillian and Hannah had fixed supper and sent Dave, Elihue's son, out to ring the dinner bell. When Clifford and Elihue didn't come, Dave and the women went into the yard and called out, yelling across the fields in their loudest farm-calling voices. No reply. Dogs barked in the distance and cowbells tinkled as the sun began to set behind Bobcat Mountain.

Just as they were about to send Ray for Martin and the neighbors to organize a search, Annie, Elihue's daughter, said, "Look, over yonder across the field." There were Clifford and Elihue, swaying toward home in the parallel rows through the cornfield, and holding hands across the young, green corn. They looked like a pair of animated scarecrows in their floppy old felt hats and red bandanas, and they sang loud and far off key:

> *Just as I am without one plea*
> *But that Thy blood was shed for me*
> *And that thou bidst me come to thee.*
> *O Lamb of God I come*

Elihue and Clifford celebrated every moment away from the hard labor of their farms, especially during the Christmas season. With all the crops in, hogs slaughtered and meat preserved, fall plowing done, and hay baled and put away, it was time to begin preparation for Christmas and the joy of freedom. The men took Elihue's wagon and mules, Maude and Henry, to Oak Hill to sell grain

17

and buy staples for Christmas and the long winter ahead.

On that cold and clear day a dense layer of frost covered every exposed surface. Up before daybreak, the two men tended to their chores before undertaking the twenty-mile trip down the old curvy road parallel to Laurel Creek. They would pass the one-room Sycamore Cove school, climb over Conley Hill, and through the tiny community of Woodleaf. Jack's Creek and Laurel Creek would join before they reached Oak Hill, the isolated county seat in the foothills of the Blue Ridge Mountains. The furniture industry and cotton mills had just begun to suck out the small farmers and all they represented from the coves and hollers, leaving farming to those such as the Fletcher brothers, who still owned large tracts of level bottom land and upland timber.

On this morning, Elihue stopped by for Clifford at about six o'clock. Climbing up onto the wide plank seat across the front of the wagon, Clifford said, "Wait jist a minute, Elihue." He crawled back down, pulled his wool coat tight, and ambled around to the back porch of his white farmhouse. A minute later he came strolling back, one hand tucked in a pocket, the other swinging a gray crockery jug by its loop handle. He handed the jug up to Elihue and crawled up. Elihue passed the jug back to Clifford, who then pulled the cork from its narrow mouth, hoisted it up on his forearm, and sucked down a drink. He handed it back to Elihue. "Needed a little something to warm us up. It's colder'n a polar bear's balls." Elihue likewise took a pull, wiped his mouth on his sleeve, and set the jug between them on the seat. After another exchange of plugs of Elihue's tobacco twist, they were ready to go.

With a snap of his wrist, Elihue started Maude and Henry on their long walk. The men didn't mind the journey except for the bumpy frozen ruts under the solid wagon wheels. The brothers, no more than two years apart and cut from the same mountain fabric, sipped and talked of harvest, complaining and bragging about that year's yield. They watched the light turn from deep purple to misty gray. The shimmering sun began breaking on the tops of the hoarfrost-covered peaks surrounding Mount Mitchell in the western distance. Maude and Henry ambled steadily on with steamy rhythmic breaths as the mountain-bound valley gave way to gray foothills. By the time they arrived at Oak Hill, the wide, frozen Main Street was bustling with merchants, peddlers, lawyers, and customers.

At the end of their jarring ride, the two men had finished half their jug. First, they sold their grain at the mill. Back on the wagon, Elihue, slurring his speech and rocking back and forth with money jingling in his pocket, told Clifford, "Foller behind me with the wagon, Cliff. Pick up the stuff I buy for Christmas."

At the first stop it was big boxes of chocolate bars; next stop, jars of jellybeans and bundles of peppermint sticks and candy canes. Elihue brought out boxes of tinsel and silvered balls for the Christmas tree, then added horehound candy and taffy, twisted ropes of black licorice, a case of Cracker Jacks, and finally, big bags filled with hard, multicolored sugar candy, orange peanut circus candy, butter mints, and lollipops. At the end of their erratic course through the streets, they had collected half a wagonload of candy and decorations in the spirit of Christmas. Somewhat bewildered by their own excess, almost out of money, and down to a third of their essential jug, they mounted the wagon and turned the mules toward home. Feeling the slackened reins, Maude and Henry instinctively plodded north toward their familiar valley and the shelter of their barn. By late afternoon the sun had evaporated the silver rime ice from the mountain tops and thawed the rutted road into twenty miles of slick red-clay mud. With about one-fourth of the jug's contents remaining, both men had nodded off, leaning on each other with a wool blanket draped across their legs. Near Flint Station Depot the road cut upstream along the steep edge of Dobson's Branch, which trickled beside them in a lush, green-draped ravine. The mules struggled in the mire of the road as it hugged the side of Buckeye Mountain. Still several miles from rest, the wagon wheels began weaving side to side, slipping toward the edge of the bank and ravine. Finally, the heavy load shifted. Its momentum pulled the staggering mules off the bank. The entire mass tipped sideways and turned over, twisting the doubletree and wagon tongue. Still pawing at the ground, the mules fell, sliding downward on their backs over wet ferns, moss, assorted dead wildflowers, and a cushion of fallen leaves. Clifford tumbled down to a soft landing in a patch of doghobble beside the trickling water.

Elihue had managed to jump off the rig before it overturned, then crawled to the edge of the road. Still dazed, he sat at the top of the bank surveying the situation through his mental fog, his tears drawing clean streaks through the mud on his face. He looked down into the branch where wagon wheels spun upside down. Bright colored candy covered the bank like spring flowers, and Maude's and Henry's mud-stained legs were kicking air. Clifford, mud-covered, came crawling up the bank.

Seeing Elihue sitting above, he hollered, "You all right, Elihue?"

Elihue replied with a quivering slur, "Yeah, Clifford,

I'm all right. But did it bust our jug?"

On another occasion, Walter Honeycutt, along with an assortment of other relatives, was visiting Hannah and Clifford for Thanksgiving dinner. Elihue, Lillian, and their strapping young boys, Saul, Dave, and Ray, were also coming. Hannah had set the table with a fat baked chicken in the middle surrounded by stuffing, green beans, mashed potatoes, fresh butter, and fluffy biscuits. Split hickory glowed and flickered in the sooty fireplace at one end of the long dining room. A blackened coffee pot perked, hanging on a hook protruding from the rockwork in the fireplace. As the family members stood around waiting for everyone to arrive, they talked about children, crops, hogs slaughtered the day before, sewing, farm machinery, and relatives. Walter and Clifford occasionally slipped away to the porch, raising the spirit of conversation, even as they lowered the level of spirits in Clifford's gray crockery jug.

Clifford threw a lanky arm over Walter's shoulder and said, "Walt, you're the best friend I ever had. Couldn't anybody have a better friend."

Walter replied, "Aw, Clifford, you're a better friend to me than I am to you; ain't no way I'm a better friend to you than you are to me."

Clifford spouted back, "Walter, don't talk like that. You're a better friend than I am."

"Cliff, don't never try to tell me I'm a better friend when you know damn good and well you're a better friend to me, always helping with crops, hog killing, hay baling..."

Walter interrupted, "You old fool, you're the one what does all the helping. Seems like I hang around watchin' you do my work, and you're loaning me your stuff all the time." The words became more flammable as the two farmers continued to pass the jug and jockey for place of lesser friend. Walter stalked back into the house, yelling, "Shut up, Clifford, leave it alone. I don't want to hear any more out of you!"

Clifford followed Walt, stepping over Old Driver, Clifford's red hound dog lying on the porch. Old Driver raised his head long enough to see what was happening as Clifford let the screen slam hard behind him. The pitch of the voices rose as they hurled insulting compliments at each other. Then things turned ugly. Clifford shoved Walter; Walter shoved back. They pushed, clawed, and wrestled around the dining room table, wallowing across a cane-bottom chair, knocking it into the fireplace and coffee pot. Hot coffee splashed out, hissing a cloud of steam from the fire. Hannah screeched as it splashed her cotton stocking-covered legs.

When Elihue, Lillian, and the boys arrived, Walter and Clifford were still pulling at each other's white Sunday shirts, worn especially for Thanksgiving. The washed and rewashed cloth easily tore into thin strips, leaving nothing but the collar and flags of frayed cloth hanging over Clifford's stout farmer torso. Blood oozed from Walter's nose, staining his shredded starched shirt. The fracas moved out to the porch, then onto the clean-swept yard. Everybody followed them, the younger children screaming with horror or delight.

Lillian helped Hannah and the other aunts round up the little ones, throwing them into the chicken lot to keep them out of harm's way while the resident chickens flapped and squawked. Elihue and the boys pulled Walter off Clifford, dragging him off to lock him in the corncrib. Old Driver, ever wise with survival skills, crept into the dining room where he propped his feet on the edge of the table.

During the ruckus, a passenger train loaded with wealthy holiday travelers heading up the mountain slowly steamed its way up the grade past this mountain family's Thanksgiving gathering. Windows dropped and heads poked out into the cool November as two grown, bloodied mountain men in shredded shirts were being dragged apart by two brawny boys. Several youngsters—some crying, some laughing and running around in a wire enclosure among a flock of terrified chickens—suggested a strange quality in Appalachian families.

Old Driver offered the travelers a final glimpse as he circled the edge of the yard and trotted across the Laurel Creek footlog in search of a quiet place to feast upon his own Thanksgiving bounty, the fat baked hen planted securely on his snout.

And that was the way Martin and Clifford and Elihue lived: hard work, hard play and hard drinking. In fact, the family has a proud heritage of excessive drinking. It has been the humor of many, the pleasure of some, and the bane of others. It has infused their lives from open gaudy excess at Christmas gatherings to secret lies, broken hearts, and financial ruin. The humor of their excesses makes the painful realities bearable.

§

Laurel Creek wasn't always gentle. Sometimes it swelled from its banks, washing away the crops and eradicating the labor of an entire season. The farmers of Sycamore Cove lived by the weather, read it with care and expertise. Their grain mills depended upon it, and they were subject to its whims. In 1916 a deluge came to the valley. The raging Laurel Creek and mountain landslides destroyed homes, killing several people. The flood washed out the supporting landfills of the newly constructed Clinchfield Railroad, leaving the rails and ties swinging in the sky, still intact like a bizarre trapeze. The flood killed Ed Simmons as he stood on the porch of his house off old Buckeye Road. A big chunk of Buckeye Mountain slid off, carrying Ed, who stood on that porch like the captain of some strange ship, into the water below.

Old Jake Conley, who had died years before the flood, was buried in the Sycamore Cove Methodist Church cemetery beside the river. His son Ned, along with family and neighbors, trudged through torrential rain up a hill on Bobcat Mountain to wait for the water to go down. The church and his house along the creek were underwater or washed away. Ned, resigned to the futility of action, sat on the high hill. With his good view of the deluge below and nothing better to do, he reasoned, why not get drunk? With a good buzz and a sense of futility at the local apocalypse, he looked toward the cemetery where his family members had been buried over the years, all now under the raging creek. "I gonny," he moaned. "Old Jake's gone to Hell, but he's in high water tonight."

Elihue's house, built right beside the creek, was washed away in the flood. With the help of his son Dave, he had carried his wife, Lillian, sitting in a rocking chair with her newborn son on her lap, through the rising floodwater to the security of a high-knolled corn crib. After the flood, with the help of his neighbors, Elihue constructed a new house on a rise near Bobcat Mountain. For the Fletcher family, the 1916 flood, forever more was a part of valley lore, setting apart the old from the new. Billy Avery would grow up hearing the story of how his father, a newborn baby, was carried to safety on his mother's lap through the torrential rain.

The valley road, crooked, simple and unpaved, snaked alongside Laurel Creek through Sycamore Cove. It had been the only way for the farmers to travel east to Oak Hill for supplies or west to the Carolina frontier with its promise of available mountain land, dramatic waterfalls, and cooler temperatures. On this road mules and horses were more reliable than Model T and Model A Fords, which mired up to their axles, requiring somebody with a team of mules to tow them out. A trip to town with a team of mules would take a good day. A better road would bring progress and a slow end to the isolation of the valley.

In the 1930s the road was moved to the middle of the valley, straightened, and paved. But the farmers didn't want change. They suspected the new road was as much about bringing tourists to the mountain town of Buckeye, with its beautiful views and spectacular Buckeye Falls, as it was about helping farmers haul their crops.

Old Ned Conley got completely outraged about state officials hard-topping the road, especially when they decided to beautify it by planting silver maples all along the new roadside. They planted hundreds of the trees from halfway to the city limits of Oak Hill to the foot of Buckeye Mountain, where the new road started its climb to Buckeye Falls.

The valley farmers depended on crops of corn, wheat, oats and soybeans. Silver maples grow large, shallow roots that spread out from the trunk, sucking up the rain and putting an end to any other plants trying to share the shade. The roots lie right under the surface of the ground. Mules, plows, and silver maple roots are natural enemies. And the roots take up valuable land where a few more rows of corn or a few more bushels of grain can grow.

Ned was a tall man, not an ounce of fat on him. He had a full shock of sandy curly hair. His face, red and sun-beaten, glowed with his Scots-Irish heritage. Other more cautious farmers considered the Scots-Irish restless and hot tempered in contrast to their own slowness to act and tendency to grumble. Ned embodied the local Scots-Irish stereotype. Rather than sitting back, he was born to start something. Knowing he'd have local support, he decided to wage war on the beautification project.

He set out to follow a few days behind the road beautification crew, digging up the little silver maples and putting them back in the same hole, with their roots waving in the air like the locks of Medusa, their little branches buried in the ground and tamped down.

After finishing his rearrangement of the state project, Ned announced to the world, "The State Highway Department don't know its ass from a hole in the ground, nor which part of a tree should go in the hole if they figured it out."

Ned's protest started the great Sycamore Cove tree rush. Folks went to the highway and absconded with the trees to set in their yards, for protest, yes, but also for shade. The state gave up the project.

Some of the silver maples survived Ned Conley. However, only a few ragged trees remain today. Their big forked branches have grown longer and heavier, cracking in lightning and wind, their symmetry gone. They are reminders of hard lives in the valley; still, they speak with the receding voices of those who handed down their stories. Billy and his brother played in the shade of those silver maples his grandparents had retrieved for the family homes.

Part 2
Jehue's Generation

Church membership was pivotal in Sycamore Cove, where everyone was expected to profess at least token acceptance of some creed. Almost all of the farmers in Sycamore Cove were Methodists, having come from English backgrounds. Scots-Irish settlers had formed a Presbyterian congregation and built a little rock church meant to last. In time, the small African-American community built an AME Zion church which also served as a school in this time of racial segregation. The Baptists were latecomers, usually merchants or railroad workers, eventually officials in the small industries that were sprouting up near Oak Hill. All of the other denominations predated the Baptists by nearly half a century, but as their numbers gradually increased, they built their own congregation, eventually naming their church The Jesus of Resurrection Free Will Baptist. The old established congregations regarded this church, which offered no historical justification for its own existence in their minds, as an upstart. Its cemetery entombed no ancestral forefathers. The few stones on its rather vacant graveyard were new and smooth and boring. Everything was new, unformed. Furthermore, services at the Jesus of the Resurrection Free Will Baptist involved whooping and hollering, loud choruses of *Amen* and *Thank you Jesus* as the congregation worked themselves into a frenzy. The sounds sometimes pierced the quiet Sunday air beyond the church walls to the horror of the more restrained (and thus more respectable) Methodists. The local gentry dubbed them Hard-Shelled Baptist, a social death sentence among the valley elite.

Staunch in their Methodist loyalty, the Fletchers glossed over the proud heritage from their forbear,

Daniel Fletcher, who for years had operated a successful distillery on Wildcat Creek, taking advantage of its clear waters coursing through Fletcher woodlands and into Laurel Creek. Elihue and Clifford had helped build Sycamore Cove Methodist church, sitting at the foot of Buckeye Mountain. Gathering rounded quartz rocks from Laurel Creek, the community had laid the four sturdy walls, later adding a tall white steeple. Cove Methodist was filled with Fletcher sons and grandsons, wives and granddaughters who married within the community fold. Eventually, Jehue Fletcher filed a request to the railroad company for the gift of a bell. He was certain that it was given because of his family prestige. The congregation stood proudly on the steps as the celebratory picture was taken.

Although his family were among the earliest settlers, Hiram Walker chose to rip up his Presbyterian roots and attend the Baptist church, thus sealing his family's fate as somewhat beneath the other valley farmers. Perhaps it was caused by the rumors surrounding Hiram's wife, who looked suspiciously Cherokee. Hiram was of Scots-Irish stock, but his wife had black hair and brown eyes. She didn't grow up in any of the nearby communities. Her origins were mysterious. Nobody knew how the marriage had happened.

In Willie Walker, their son, Jehue Fletcher found a friend. Too young to find companionship in his older brothers, he drifted up and down the valley looking for a playmate, a companion in his lonely early years. He was a country boy, allowed to ramble in the valley while the family was busy with never-ending chores. He had heard his parents speak in vague references to the Walkers, who lived about a mile up the road, but he was too young to pay attention to conversations. The two kids became fast friends, roaming the woods, swimming in Laurel Creek, building play forts in the woods, laughing and sharing secrets. Both kids were isolated: Jehue by his youth and the work ethic of his family, Willie by social ostracism and the loneliness of an only child.

As Jehue and Willie grew up, both were kept busy by work on their family farms. Nobody was exempt from farm work, and both boys quickly grew into more demanding and time-consuming tasks, Jehue under Elihue's heavy thumb, and Willie, who took on more and more as his grandfather stiffened with age. As he grew up, Jehue learned to understand social status and to adhere to family norms. Willie's innate tendency toward isolation, his family's church choice, and his questioning mind in this tight and doctrinaire community combined to distance the two boys from one another.

At school, Willie just didn't fit in. He was quiet and reserved. The other boys seemed a little afraid of him, and, indifferent to popularity, he never pursued their friendship or participated in school activities. Jehue, on the other hand, was an outgoing kid who wanted to be accepted. He joked with his classmates, tagged along with them, jumped at the chance to be involved. Willie was left behind. The two naturally drifted apart into a casual friendliness. Although Willie made good grades, he quit school when he turned fifteen, under the pretense of being needed on his grandfather's farm.

He also quit going to church with his parents, who never missed a service, a Bible study, an opportunity to rededicate themselves to Jesus, and who urged him to do likewise. Willie simply refused to go, unmoved by his parents' pleas and prayers. Although he loved music, he found nothing beautiful in loud shouts, testimonies, and endless verses of off-key altar calls. Occasionally he would approach a church regular with questions about religion, usually involving Biblical inerrancy. The friendly farmer at a cornshucking would be confronted with sudden questions about his own beliefs, especially regarding the existence of a hereafter. The men huddled around the stove at Homer Waycaster's store would be interrupted in their easy comradery with an explosive compulsive remark unrelated to the conversation at hand. "I been wondering about God wiping out all them cities just because a few people done too much drinking and carousing. Besides that, Jesus made extra wine for that wedding. You'd think he wouldn't do that if it was so bad to have a few drinks. Maybe he wanted a little more hisself." Some of the local derelicts would hide their smiles, but the righteous were disturbed. It was heresy in the shape of a dark-eyed boy, and the upright churchgoers would try to straighten him out by bombarding him with clichés. Their answers were never satisfactory.

He read the Bible from cover to cover more than once. As he grew older, still with his unsettling questions, most people began avoiding him. "They ain't enough water to cover the earth above all the mountains," he would say. Or "Galileo was put in prison for saying that the earth went around the sun when the Bible says it's the other way around." And, "Who did Cain marry if him and Abel was the only two young'uns of Adam and Eve?"

The row of men sat on milking stools, cane bottom chairs, and wooden crates in the barn loft, talking in voices that were swallowed by the darkness around them. Their hands worked with practiced rhythm, stripping away the shucks, tossing the glowing ears of corn in a slatted plank bin, and throwing the frayed chattering shucks behind them into a great pile. There would be no waste; the corn would sustain cattle and family through the long Blue Ridge Mountain winter. The shucks would feed livestock and serve as bedding for young calves. Most families, however, had passed the time when shucks filled the ticking of beds that now offered the warmth of goose down.

"Seen any wooly worms this fall, Delo?" asked Wade Baucom, a short, bald man in overalls and a plaid wool coat. Wade sat next to Delo on a weathered apple crate, his girth obstructing his working hands.

"I seen two or three. They was all black on each end and brown in the middle," Delo said, not looking up from his work. "Guess it's gonna get bad soon. But if them wooly buggers is right, Christmas should be right nice."

Delo Fletcher, Elihue's cousin, looked like the Fletchers. He was the physical opposite of Wade—tall, lean and muscular. His face was long and narrow, matching his nose, but his ears were big enough to be comical. He sat working his long fingers with an efficiency that Wade couldn't possibly match.

"That's good if you put any stock in wooly worm perdictions. That front-end cold spell ought to come about Thanksgiving, hog killing time." Wade worked his stubby thumb against an ear, ripping it open with his shucking tool. "I always worry that it's gonna be too warm, lose some meat before we get it salted and put away," said Wade. "I don't really put no stock in wooly worms. Now the *Farmer's Almanac* and the signs is what I go by. It's done right by my crops for years. My momma made me do everthing by the signs. I got to doin' it that way and it's worked right by me so far."

In the big weathered barn, bins were filled on one side with ears of dry corn pressing against the inside of their pale shucks with brown silks hanging from each ear. Other bins held the fat corn already shucked. It was night, and a row of kerosene lanterns hanging from the rafters yielded soft golden light, warming the early fall night, providing just enough light to tame the darkness of the cavernous old barn. It was a scene that had played out for over a century.

Delo said "Yep" and kept on working. "Lotta work to be done."

"Why don't them Fletcher boys come help you out, being you're cousins and all?" said Wade.

"Aw, they're shucking down at Elihue's tonight. Knowin' that bunch, there'll be about as much drinkin' as working. It'll take the whole lot of 'em to get through the corn and shine," said Delo.

"Seems like they coulda spared Jehue or Ray. Guess they wouldn't want to miss out on the family shenanigans, though. By the way, speaking of shine, it feels a little drafty up here without my hat on, Delo," said Wade. "Got a little something to warm us up?"

"Here, take it easy on this stuff. We have to keep our wits, get this shucking done," said Delo, pulling a green pint mason jar out of the bin in front of him. "I ain't goin' home lit having these younguns with us. Edna would shell my nuts. Them kids begged so much, and they love to play in the shucks. I just had to let them come, plenty of us to watch out for them. You better be heedful of Hattie too, if you think we're gonna drain that jar."

"I seen Edner over here canning almost ever day. Glad she's got that fire pit you built her so she wouldn't have to stay in the house against a hot cook stove all summer. Reckon we could build one for Hattie before next summer, Delo? She's about cooked herself this year."

"Why don't you build her one yourself. You've got enough rocks out of your fields to make her a goodun," Delo said.

"I ain't never been no good with fittin' rocks together, nor making mortar so it will stay put. Why, if I built one myself, it'd fall apart the first time Hattie built a fire in it," Wade said. "You Fletchers have that rock-layin' in your blood. Look at what old Elihue and Clifford done; they laid about half the rock out there at Laurel Creek Methodist. Got the rocks for the whole thing outta the creek. That church'll stand for centuries. That's one fine piece of work."

"Well, I tell you, Wade. I'll help you if you'll quit running your mouth and get this shucking done."

"I believe we've got a deal, Delo," Wade chuckled.

The men wore caps or straw hats during the day but sat bare headed so they could see by the dim light from overhead. Delo had a shock of unruly gray hair that seemed to be enjoying its freedom. Down the row sat Cletus Denny, a boy who had been hanging around Delo's daughter, Maggie, a little too much for Delo's comfort. But this night Delo needed all hands to finish the job. Cletus sat beside an empty chair he'd put where his daddy used to sit. Next to Cletus was Anvil Burch, a work-hardened, thick-boned young man in his twenties, strongest of the lot but slow at corn shucking. His daddy had named him Anvil because he said a name like that would make him tough, somebody who could take the hits.

Wade leaned over toward Delo and spoke quietly. "You reckon that Anvil will ever make anything of himself? He's about as quick witted as molasses in the winter."

"Don't reckon it's much of my business," said Delo. "He'll be whatever he'll be. Choice is his and God's to make."

"God ain't got no hand in it. Anvil don't never go to church. You'd think his momma would make him go," Wade said. "But, you know, his momma stopped going too after the explosion."

"Well, when you lose your daddy like he done, it's gotta be hard. Maybe he'll start back after he's done grieving," Delo replied. "You never know." That limestone mine's claimed more'n one life since it opened. Owners don't live here and don't care as long as they get their money."

"Hey, Anvil, when you gonna come back to church?" asked Wade.

Anvil stopped his slow-motion shucking. "Ain't comin' back."

"You'll go to Hell if you don't. You ought to come on back and bring your momma."

"Ain't none of your business," said Anvil.

"Just askin', just askin'. Preacher says we're supposed to try to bring the sheep into the fold," Delo said.

"I ain't no sheep, Delo. And they ain't no God," said Anvil.

Everybody stopped shucking and looked at Anvil. "Anvil, that's blasphemy," said Cletus. "You ought not to say such a thing." Delo felt a little better about Cletus for firing back at Anvil.

"After what happened to daddy, how can I believe they's a God. My daddy was a good man. He took care of our family, went to church, made us say the blessing before we eat. He even made us git down on our knees beside the bed and say our prayers," Anvil said.

"Ours ain't to question the ways of God," said Wade. "He had a purpose. Maybe he needed your daddy up in Heaven. Why, God may even use explosive experts up there. We don't know."

"That's the silliest thing I've ever heard," said Delo. "Ain't a man alive what knows why a good man like that gets killed. And, what about all them men that was killed in the big war. I don't think God wanted them killed.

"Delo, God knows everthing that's happened, is happening and is gonna happen," said Wade, pointing his shucking tool upward.

"If that's true, why do we bother worrying about doing anything?" asked Cletus. Delo's face dropped. Cletus was thinking too much. "We need to drop this and get the shucking done or we won't get a wink of sleep tonight," he said.

The men quietly resumed their work, only the chatter of dry shucks breaking the silence.

"Why lookie down there, if that Cletus ain't done found a red ear," said Wade. Cletus tried to hide the ear, but it was too late. "You know what that means."

"Don't mean nothing," Cletus said. "All that stuff's just superstition. Just like them wooly worms. You don't actually believe that the color of a wooly worm can tell what kind of winter we're going to have, do you?"

"Well, son, they's lots we don't understand," Wade said. "I've seen some things come true. Like last year they wasn't a handful of acorns off the oak trees, and it was a

37

tame winter just like the old saying goes."

"I don't believe none of that stuff. How can anything tell what ain't happened yet?" Cletus said.

"You believe in Heaven and Hell don't you, Cletus?" asked Wade.

"Of course." Cletus replied.

"You're full of crap, Cletus," said Anvil. "They ain't no pearly gates. Why do you believe that stuff?"

"Because the Bible says it," Cletus replied.

"It's a book, wrote by old men who wanted to keep people under control. Scare the Hell out of them, or more likely into them so they would do whatever they was told," said Anvil. "And it's working, ain't it?"

"Anvil Burch, you stop that kind of talk before lightning strikes this barn," said Wade.

"Okay everbody, here we go again," said Delo. "This ain't getting' the shucking done. "Besides, we ought to be happy to think that Cletus'll find hisself a pretty brown-haired wife, just like the red ear predicts." Delo's daughter had sandy-blond hair.

They returned to their task. When most of the shucking was done, Delo said, "It's quittin' time boys. I can get the rest of it from here. Things will be a little slow around here since the crops and hay are in. Guess we'll be over at Wade's barn in a day or two."

"See," said Wade. "We do know what's going to happen in the future. My corn's gonna get shucked. And Anvil there is going to Hell." They all laughed as they put on their hats and shoved their shucking tools into their pockets.

Delo and Wade picked up two sleeping children from the shuck pile. Cletus and Anvil took down two lanterns, each making their way down the ladder, through the wide alley of the barn and across the pasture. Delo and

Wade, each carefully carrying a child, negotiated their way across the footlog over the soft whispering Tunnel Branch. They trudged up the slope to the big white farm house on a knoll beside great bare grain fields.

"Well, it's about time," said Hattie. "What you boys been doin' down there? You don't need to tell me. You was flappin' your jaws more than you was shucking corn. Come on in to the kitchen after you put them babies to bed."

"It's eleven o'clock boys, but you have to have your hot chocolate," said Edna. "Can't break tradition. Shame them little ones fell asleep. I'll give them some in the morning."

Bastard

On the fourth day after Lillian had told Elihue about Sarah's baby, he looked up from his dinner plate and said, "Don't nobody leave the table. I've got something to say." They had eaten in silence. He had kept his head down, shoveling his food with purpose. His demeanor was different; it smothered all hunger. He'd cleaned his plate with the last biscuit scrap before finishing off his glass of buttermilk. After shoving his plate away, he leaned back in the cane bottom chair, resting his big hands on the table.

"By now all of you know your sister's got herself biggered by Morris Clark. We've tried to raise you younguns right. Your momma and me's told you right from wrong." He lowered his head then raised his eyes, measuring each of his children. "They's a price to be paid for sin, and I ain't lettin' sin into this house. They ain't no judge and jury, no law here except the law of God and my law as man of this house, and judgement is due. He paused, pulled out his tobacco pouch, rolled a cigarette and lit it. He took a deep draw. "All of you go out in the backyard, right now, all except Momma."

No one moved until he stormed, "Right now, out, all of you!"

They jumped to their feet, running out the kitchen door and down the steps to the clean-swept backyard. The chickens flapped away into the brown cornstalks in the field. Annie held on to Sarah's arm, and the five boys huddled against the house whispering to each other. The day was bright and cold. Even without their coats, no one noticed the chill. Elihue came, long and lean, down the steps. He put his old felt hat on his bald head, flipped his cigarette into the yard, and walked to the smokehouse a few steps away. He came back with six thick maple sticks, peeled of their bark, smooth white, all about an arm's length. He passed them to each of the boys and brought one to Annie. And he held another one that was thicker and longer than the others.

"Get in a straight line, side by side down through yonder." He pointed across the yard.

They shuffled into the yard, Elihue grabbing Jehue by the shoulders and shoving him into place. He was the youngest, the baby, eleven years old.

"Line up beside Jehue, about a yard apart," Elihue said.

Dave, the oldest at nineteen, stepped beside Jehue. Ray, the heaviest brother, was next. Sammy, only one year younger than Sarah, moved into place. Saul, the one everybody said was the most like Elihue, took Annie's arm and pulled her beside him into the last place. They all stared down at the ground, only glancing at Elihue, who had grabbed Sarah's arm and pulled her to stand in front of Jehue.

"Look at her, Jehue! Did she do something wrong?"

"Yessir," Jehue said quietly. He didn't look at Sarah.

"People that do something as bad as your sister done has got to be punished. Ain't that right boy?"

"I guess so."

"You guess so? You mean you know so."

"Yessir."

"Yessir what?"

"She's gotta be punished."

"That's right, she's gotta be punished for fornicating." Turning to Sarah, Elihue said, "You stand right here girl."

He paced along the row of his children, catching each with a stern, cold stare before stopping in front of Sarah. "Jehue! You strike her in the belly with that stick

41

and strike hard. Ain't no bastard going to grow up on my farm!"

Jehue looked down the line at all the others and didn't move. "You strike her or I'll take my stick to you. I'm gonna teach all of you there's a price to pay for fornication, for disobeying me. Now hit her!"

Sarah turned to run. Elihue grabbed her with his long arm. "You stand still girl or I'll be the one to lay into you. I'll hit you twice as hard as Jehue or any of the others." Sarah began to cry, clutching her stomach. "Take your hands away from your belly, girl."

He grabbed Jehue's hand, drew back the club and slammed it across her stomach. The sting and force shocked her. As she bent forward, her knees buckled. She gasped for breath, crying out.

"Stand up girl, or I'll have my go at you. Move down the line." He pulled her up, then shoved her with his powerful hand. "Dave, you know what to do. Don't hold back or you'll get the rod from me." He pulled Sarah's arms behind her back.

Tears welled in Dave's eyes as he drew back his stick and slammed it across Sarah's writhing unborn child. Crying, Sarah fell away gasping for breath. Her legs failed again, but Elihue lifted her up, cinched her hands behind her back, and pushed her down the line. He forced each trembling boy to slam her across the stomach, even as she twisted in agony.

Sammy held back the force of his blow, tears streaming down his red, round cheeks. Elihue slammed him across the shoulder. "Again! Harder this time!" Sammy did as his father commanded, then Saul took his turn with full force. Annie sobbed as she struck Sarah, not as hard as the others. Elihue made her hit with force enough to send his message: *"You'll not do what she did."*

The gauntlet started again with Jehue. Sarah heaved and vomited, saw the blood oozing through her dress. By the third pass of the line, as she reached Annie, she felt heat streaming down her legs. The red stain ran across her shoes, soaking into the pale, dry dirt. The world disappeared, the pain gone. She awoke in bed. Lillian held a cool wet cloth on her head. She had undressed her daughter, salved the stinging abrasions on her stomach, and washed her. Sarah's flat belly was deep blue.

She agonized through uncounted hours as the pain slowly drove away the dreams, as the bleeding stopped soaking the sackcloths her mother silently changed each day. She watched her plum-blue belly turn to green and yellow as the bruises faded. She cried out when her mother and Annie helped her to the chamber pot. Their touch was tender, but their silence echoed her father's rigid words.

"She is no longer your daughter or your sister. She can live here till her and the boys build her and that son-of-a-bitch a shack somewhere nobody has to see them much, maybe in that hole on the branch beside the cemetery. That way she'll be reminded ever day what she done."

Sarah had never really known Elihue. He had paid most of his attention to the boys because they helped him work the farm. She had seen him whip her brothers with his razor strop until their legs bled, but she was stunned by what he had done to her. Annie had warned her, saying, "There's no telling what Daddy will do when he finds out. You know how he feels; he calls girls whores that get pregnant before they've married." But Sarah had thought she and Morris could quietly get married before the baby came; he had a job at the quarry, they could make do. It would be simple.

Now she remembered all of it, how her father's cold eyes had blazed through her when her mother told him after supper three weeks ago. How three days passed before he even said anything except to bark orders to Momma and the boys about how much work had to be done on the farm before winter set in hard in the valley. The silence was terrible. He passed her without a word, without a glance. She should have known.

Sarah and Morris were quietly married in Elihue's house. He and Lillian served as witnesses. Elihue's stern face was a testimony to his unforgiving resolve. Elihue, his brothers and older sons had built a rude two room shack in a worthless swale below the family cemetery.

Through the years Elihue's grandchildren heard only whispers of what had happened on that cold day. All they knew was that Aunt Sarah and Uncle Morris didn't have nearly as much as other family members. The farm remained the center of their lives. Elihue continued to run the best farm in the valley, his soil black and deep. But one small unmarked fieldstone shadow on his land grew longer.

The family expanded to include in-laws and grandchildren. Sons married, moved to nearby homes. Billy Fletcher would remember the warm Christmas holidays when Elihue's sons, their wives and the grandchildren moved back to the old home for days of Christmas love. It was a time for decorating, cooking, drinking, and the ritual fireworks of Christmas Eve. Sarah's resolve was to never allow her pain to show in Elihue's presence. She steeled herself, becoming beloved by the grandchildren and wives of her brothers. She shared their whiskey bottles and displayed a bold irreverence at the raucous gatherings. She endured.

True, the small depot in Sycamore Cove bore the name of Buckeye, but that was about politics, not geography. The station was there to serve the wealthy who summered in the resort town of Buckeye, fifteen miles north in the higher, cooler mountains. The rich summer residents and the people who served them wanted the name recognition of Buckeye rather than the name of a mundane farm community. Still, Sycamore Cove residents enjoyed the convenience of catching the train to anywhere from that isolated station.

The Fletcher family had a very different purpose for the trains. They used them to get fireworks, which were illegal in North Carolina. They ordered large shipments brought in from Panther Fireworks Company in Ohio. Men and boys saved their money all year and poured over the Panther catalog for their Christmas order; they bought fireworks by the gross, even by the case. Excitement built for weeks until the train brought the prized cargo.

The Christmas fireworks, showering bright fountains, spinning pinwheels of blazing sparks, painted color onto the sky. The startling reports of M80s, double shots, aerial and cherry bombs, were shared by the whole valley. But Jehue, never content with his own fireworks, always wanted the biggest, loudest aerial bomb available, perhaps because he was the youngest, the smallest of five brothers, the one who wore glasses, the pampered pet of his mother and his sister Annie.

Searching all of the fireworks catalogs, Jehue aimed for the pinnacle of power and percussion. He found it.

Everyone would know that it was Jehue Fletcher's big red ten-dollar aerial bomb that shattered the valley silence from one thousand feet above. It stood eighteen inches high with a diameter of four inches, a five-inch fuse and a six-inch-square wooden base. It was magnificent, made by Red Cat Fireworks in Akron, Ohio. The money Jehue saved for it would have bought a large assortment of Roman candles, rockets, double shots, pinwheels, fountains, ladyfingers, side loaders, cherry bombs, and gray-fused firecrackers that came in packs that could be lighted all at once. Instead, all of his money went for the big show, for his proclamation of power.

He was at the depot early each day, sitting on one of the big green freight wagons on the platform beside the tracks. Finally, one day the train hissed to a stop and Pete Brown, the station master, disappeared into the darkness of a red boxcar, returning with a single box labeled, "To JEHUE FLETCHER from "RED CAT FIREWORKS." Jehue's heart thumped as he gently carried the box away.

Everyone always converged at Elihue and Lillian's house for Christmas celebrations—Santa Claus, mountains of food, bourbon, and gifts, the mayhem lasting for days. Christmas Eve was fireworks night. This year, after all the Roman candles, the fountains, the pinwheels, and rockets, Jehue would provide a singular grand finale. With his aerial bomb, he would put the capstone on the Christmas Eve show.

The big night came, fireworks had lit up the evening, and now his audience was ready. Jehue took the marvel a safe distance from the house, placing it on the ground with its red shaft pointing menacingly skyward. He struck the match. "Take cover, men!" The flame touched the thick fuse. "Tssssss," it ignited. With fingers stuck in their ears, men and children scattered behind the well house, into the smoke house, behind the woodpile, under dense boxwoods, and behind the lattice under the porch. The women squinted into the darkness through the windows. Silence thick with expectation pierced the dark. Straining eyes could see the dim fuse sputtering into the cold night air.

The hissing of the fuse was broken by a quiet "pfff-ttt"—so was Jehue's spirit, as a puff of smoke weakly ejaculated from the big red cylinder. The silence was soon broken by the humiliation heaped upon him by his brothers.

Determined, Jehue turned to dynamite during the remaining celebration days. He began detonating whole sticks he hung from low limbs of trees on the hill above the house. Windows rattled for miles up and down the valley, deep rumbles bounced between Buckeye and Wildcat Mountains. Shattered scrub pine limbs and compliments from all were testaments to his revenge on the Red Cat Fireworks Company of Akron, Ohio.

George "Boney" McGee often joined the Fletcher Christmas fireworks tradition. One crisp December day, he and his wife, Erlene, were coming to visit Elihue and Lillian in their Model A coupe. Ray Fletcher was on his way too, walking just up the road. Boney and Erlene were rattling along in their car when they saw Ray. Boney, who liked practical jokes, decided to throw a cherry bomb out of the Model A window as they neared.

Erlene struck the match, the joy of anticipation causing her and Boney to laugh in anticipation of their prank. Boney slowed down, held the fuse to the match, and pitched the bomb with its sizzling stem toward Ray. One minor detail had been forgotten. The window in the car was still rolled up against the cold wind. The cherry bomb bounced off the window, fussing around inside the car as though it knew what devilish deed it was about to do.

Suddenly, a subdued metallic sound, "FRANKK," tore through the air as the exploding bomb jabbed against the sheet metal inside the little coupe. A blue translucent cloud filled the inside of the car, pressing against the windows. The Ford veered off the road and into the grain stubble, doors springing open like the wings of a scared chicken. Boney and Erlene rolled awkwardly onto the ground as the Ford squirmed to a driverless stop. The ringing in their ears and a few scratches and scrapes were embarrassing reminders of their holiday prank gone wrong.

Billy always remembered those feelings of connection with cousins and uncles as they set off fireworks on the edge of his grandfather's field in those last days of the big family farm. Roman candles cradled in little hands held gently by the leathery farm-worked hands of family men sent spheres of colored light into the valley darkness on Christmas Eve. The bright joy bound together uncles, aunts, and cousins—a fresh-cut cedar tree, aromas from the kitchen, laughter at enduring stories, and finally, a deep feather bed with visions of fireworks arching into the night linger across the decades.

The long cold winter settled over Sycamore Cove after the Christmas celebrations ended. Evergreen hemlocks and pines contrasting with gray, leafless oak, maple and the remaining chestnut trees lent a solemnity to the surrounding mountain landscape. Deep quilts of snows would cover the barren, sleeping fields awaiting another season of fecundity. The valley would remain quiet as families tended livestock, mended the wear of hard work, stitched new Dutch doll, butterfly and nine patch quilts, consumed the harvest, and sat by warm fires in quiet reflection, sometimes sharing stories and songs passed down from the dead.

Willie Walker watched as Ezra Murphy stood in the middle of the highway with the burdensome corn sheller on his back. He was borrowing it from the Fletchers to shell his own small crop. Ezra lived on a patch of flat land in a hollow on Bobcat Mountain, above the vast acreage of the Fletcher's farm. He would carry the sheller from Elihue's granary, across the road, through Fletcher fields, across the railroad track, up the hollow, and finally to his little shack. There was no road to the crude house his father had built from planks of a deserted lumber camp, only the path worn by Ezra's family and his father before him.

Ezra, his sizable wife Evelene, and their three daughters shared the one-room house. The two presented a near-comic contrast. Ezra was short and stout; Evelene was a tall and heavy woman whose size defined her role as ruler of the household. Willie watched as Ezra stood stoop-shouldered, balancing the time-worn corn sheller with its many jabbing parts as if he hardly noticed the load on his back.

Willie felt a kinship with Ezra. They were both outsiders, Willie with his dark skin and challenges to all Sycamore Cove social conventions, Ezra with his own kind of isolation, separated from the valley's powerful by race and poverty. He worked for the local farmers, including the Fletchers and Walkers. Such work was almost all that was left for black families who wanted to remain in the cove. Ezra liked his place, working his scrap of ground, raising his girls in a quiet spot with a view of Buckeye Mountain across the valley.

Willie's grandfather had helped Ezra put a floor in the shack, which sometimes flooded in heavy rains. Now it balanced above the ground, which once had served as the floor, on stacks of flat rocks carried up from the creek, The family had wallpapered the interior with newspaper and tarpapered the outside with quarter-sized roofing nails.

Willie liked Ezra and his whole family; their music somehow vocalized what he could never say. Ezra could play any instrument available, from the big black upright piano which dominated the one-room shack to the cheap mail-order guitar and fretless banjo with its groundhog skin head. No matter the instrument, Ezra never missed a note. He could frail that old banjo till it seemed to be playing itself. He and Evelene sang and harmonized with force and beauty. Every Sunday they raised their voices in Mountain View AME Church.

Willie wished that he could go to their church for the music. He had grown up in the Jesus of the Resurrection Baptist Church, where the preacher had hardly tolerated any kind of music except the slow mournful hymns of earthly doom and calls for repentance. Willie had ceased attending once he was able to earn his own money working for his grandfather and doing odd jobs. He had hated the congregational antics—jumping onto pews, the bellicose *amens*, the fervor of whoops and moans in response to the preacher's revved-up rantings, and he had no use for the preacher himself. Willie just couldn't see Jesus in that frenzied chaos.

As time passed, he had found the literal Biblical interpretations illogical, but he liked to walk up the railroad tracks on Sundays, sit on a cut bank near the church, and listen to the old spiritual songs coming from Mountain View AME. He listened to Ezra pick that sweet gospel

music on his flat top guitar. When Ezra sang with Evelene, his daughters joining in as backup, Willie felt as
if the chariots were coming down. Only then could he
find himself approaching any condition of near-belief.
Their songs bypassed the doubt and soaked right into
his bones. He always left before the end of the long services because he didn't want the faithful to think he was
intruding on their sacred and private celebration. They
lived and worshipped in an isolated community that
Willie understood.

The state had refused to pay for a teacher to come
to the cove for a handful of black children. The nearest
black school was in Oak Hill, sixteen miles away. Homer
Hollifield, one of Willie's cousins, picked up the few remaining black children of Sycamore Cove in his old van
and drove them to school in Oak Hill. Willie, like some
of the others, had considered leaving, but the land held
him. He was committed to helping his aging grandfather maintain the farm and he loved the valley. It was
where he belonged.

Ezra, with the corn sheller on his back, had started
home when he encountered Saul Fletcher walking back
from the store. The long and winding conversation en-
sued right there in the middle of the road. They shared
opinions about the weather, everybody's health, the rest-
lessness across the ocean in those far-away countries, the
state of this year's wheat, corn, and hay, the way God
had blessed everybody so much. Willie, sitting on the cut
bank, noticed that Saul did most of the talking.

Finally, Ezra told Saul about the snake that got in the
newspapered wall the other day while the family was eat-
ing supper. One of his girls noticed a squirming in the
wallpaper, under the obituary page. Ezra reached over
and stabbed it with his fork. The blacksnake gave one

52

shudder and dropped down, ripping out of the newspaper onto the floor. Ezra said he quit supper long enough to pitch it out in the yard. Saul laughed and so did Ezra.

When Saul finally noticed that Ezra had been standing there all that time with the corn sheller on his back, he suggested that Ezra set it down. But Ezra said it would be too much trouble to pick it back up again. As the laughter drifted upward, Willie thought about Ezra, the world he held on his back, that frail shack up in the hollow, those children he was sending to school, Evelene, who helped out the farm wives, often without pay if she knew somebody was hard up for cash. She'd get paid with a ham, a jar of honey, and good will.

Willie thought of all he'd heard over the years, the stories and jokes shared between his own father and Saul Fletcher, talk centered on Ezra and his kin. He thought of the Sunday dinners of his childhood when the blessing was often followed by a joke about Ezra or one of the other black families living in the cove. Strange, he thought, the families calling the blacks ugly names, making jokes at their expense; yet, in the next breath declaring there to be no better man than Ezra, not a better woman than Evelene, always there when needed.

Ward Denny leaned back on Homer Waycaster's General Store loafers' bench and put his feet up on a cane bottom chair he'd slid around in front of him. The day was hot, but a breeze was blowing up the valley, further cooling the store's shaded porch. "Have you ever seen Ed Benfield completely sober?" he asked Bryce Wilson, who leaned forward, cutting white shavings from a maple walking stick.

"Don't know as I have; it's hard to tell with him. But you can count on one thing; he'd be up to no good, sober as a preacher or drunk as a cider gnat."

"There he goes, tromping away like usual; nothing easy about his comin' or goin'." Ward said. "I wonder what that old son-of-a-bitch'll be up to next." They watched as the lumbering figure headed south, disappearing around a bend on the dirt side road.

Zachariah, Gertie and Joshua Murphy walked south from their father's home just up the dusty road that paralleled Laurel Creek. Doug and Milo, the Willis brothers, joined them from their house in a hollow across the valley. During the dog days, it was easier to bathe and cool off in the creek than to carry water from the spring to fill the big galvanized tub at home.

"Hey Gertie, you work for Miz Baucom today?" asked Doug as he and Milo caught up with the Murphys. "Yeah, I washed clothes till I rubbed my hands raw. What you lazy boys do today, find somers to lay around sleep under a shade tree?"

"Look here, girl," Milo said, walking backwards. He leaned his head toward Gertie. "You see all this dirt in my hair and these blisters on my hands? We been puttin' up hay all day for Mister Byrd. That's one hot job. What did Zach do today? Nothing!"

Milo was a small but hardened young man of eighteen. Doug was older, maybe twenty-one, slimmer than Milo. Both were lean with tight muscles and a number of prominent scars that revealed hard work, hard living and hard playing. Both had dropped out of school as well as out of the AME Church, the core of their community.

Gertie slapped Milo on the head and said, "Zach work too hard for too little carrying that leftover slop from old man Benfield's still to feed his hogs. I told Zachariah he shouldn't be messin' with that man, didn't I Zach?" Zachariah didn't reply, just kept scuffing along the dusty road. "But it's about the onliest way he can earn a few pennies round here."

The year was 1936. Zachariah was twenty-one years old, large and strong, but with a soft, round face and big eyes. His mother had never let him go to school since there were no special resources that would help him keep up. Gertie, Zachariah's little sister, was only thirteen. She loved Zachariah, caring for him as though he were her big protective doll. Joshua, frail and thin but bright, was fifteen. The Willis brothers were about the same age as Zachariah. He idolized the brothers and followed them whenever they would let him.

The five turned off the dusty road on a path leading through a copse to the clear cool water of the creek behind Cecil Byrd's barn, where a natural flow of the water had carved out a large, still pool. A gentle cascade fell into the shallow upstream end, which gradually deepened.

The boys unbuckled and dropped their patched overalls. Gertie stripped her loose, flour-sack print dress over her head, throwing it on an alder bush. She and Zachariah waded, hand in hand, into the swimming hole. The other boys dived from a rock into the deep end of the clear pool where brook trout flashed for cover and leaf-filtered sunlight played like fairies on the ripples.

Gertie squealed when Zachariah splashed the cold mountain water over her, hard work and worry drifting away with the current of the creek. They laughed and played, slapping at water striders skating away from reach. Even the older boys returned to their happy younger years when they had felt safe and comfortable in their world. Joshua saw a small, harmless water snake slither into the water downstream. He said nothing, for he knew Gertie would scream and the Willis brothers would try to catch it to further terrify her and Zachariah. He wanted nothing to cast shadows over their moment of peace, rest, and joy.

When Ed Benfield suddenly appeared like a nightmare on the creek bank, all the joy fell away. Gertie and Zachariah, standing in the slow current, silently faced the imposing figure. Milo and Doug swam from the deep water to join them. Benfield was clad in overalls which hung loose over his hairy shirtless torso. His round head sat like a bell on his muscular frame. The remains of once sandy hair trailed into the gray stubble on his square jaw and sagging chin. He stood strong on the creek bank with his sun-baked balding head cocked slightly sideways, hands clasped under the paunch that pressed against the waist of his overalls. Stripped down and naked, the four young bathers were left vulnerable to Benfield's seething stare. Gertie clutched her knobby new breasts with her arms, turned her back to Benfield, and squatted down in the water.

"What the hell's going on here?" Benfield roared.

57

"You're on Mr. Byrd's land. This is his damn creek down here, and you're messin' up his water with nigger sweat and dirt. He's got me looking after his place, and I'm not letting any niggers come around less they're working the fields or shovelin' cow shit out of his barn."

Joshua said, "But we just washin' off, and Mr. Byrd, he said…"

"The hell, *I said* you ain't got no business in the creek. You don't talk back to a white man." He stepped forward, hoisted his worn brogan upon a rock, and leaned forward, pointing his finger at Zachariah. "I had my gun they'd be nigger blood in that water!"

"We getting out Mr. Benfield. We don't want no trouble," said Milo, wading out to the other side of the creek near the road, Doug following. Zachariah, standing motionless nearest to Benfield, stared blankly at the big white man. Joshua edged closer to retrieve Zachariah, but Benfield sloshed into the water, grabbing Joshua by the arm before he could reach Zachariah. Jerking him into his massive body, Benfield locked the boy around the throat before shoving him under the cold water. Joshua struggled back to his feet, gasping for air. Again Benfield shoved him under and held tight. Zachariah saw Joshua's thin limbs flailing. Lunging at Benfield, he knocked the big man off of Joshua, who caught his footing on the rocky creek bottom and sloshed about in the water, coughing and gasping for breath. Benfield lost his balance and sprawled into the current. Zachariah pulled Joshua to the opposite side of the creek and onto the bank while Benfield regained his footing.

The five stood tight on the opposite side of the creek. Gertie began running to the road trying to pull her dress over her head. Joshua grabbed his overalls, not even trying to put them on, and ran after her, crying, "Gertie,

wait for me! Git your overalls and come on Zach, hurry!"
The others grabbed their clothes from the nearby alder
bushes and began tugging them on their wet bodies.
Ed Benfield had climbed out of the water, stood in his
soaked overalls, staring across the creek at the terrified
group.

"Zachariah, you're going to pay for what you done!
You just wait. You ain't going to know when it's coming,
but you are going to pay like a hog at first frost for at-
tacking a white man!" He turned and walked away, disappearing through the thicket.

The Willis boys finished hitching up their overalls
and walked quietly together northward toward the Murphy home. Gertie and Joshua stopped a safe distance up
the road to wait for them. Benfield, muttering, slopped
his way back along the cattle path leading from the creek.
Gertie, Joshua and the Willis boys walked together.
Zachariah scuffed along a few yards behind, thinking
about the supper his momma would have waiting.

"Zachariah, you in trouble now! Mr. Benfield gonna
kill you! That man's mean and he do what he say he
gonna do," Milo warned.

"Now what's that fool boy gonna do? Ain't nothin' he can. Everybody's afraid of Benfield. Even white
folks scared of him when he drunk," said Doug Willis.
"You better hightail it outa this cove Zachariah. He ain't
gonna bother Milo and me cause we works on his place
and drinks peach wine with him sometimes."

"He ain't got nowheres he can go Mr. Benfield can't
find him. He better stay home and hope his momma and
daddy can stall off that old man till he cool down," Milo
said. "Besides, Zachariah can't do for hisself."

"Mr. Benfield don't never cool down. He gonna do
what he say he gonna do," said Doug. "Ain't nothin' we

can do. Zachariah dead unless somethin' happen to Mr. Benfield."

"I wish somebody'd kill him. If they don't, he gonna kill Zachariah and maybe even us too someday if we says 'hello' to him the wrong way," Milo said. Turning and walking backward, looking at Zachariah, he added, "You kill him, Zachariah; you're the one he real mad at."

"I can't kill nobody. Besides, Mr. Benfield makes me work for him," said Zachariah. "I kill him he won't give me any of his whiskey. He sometimes give me a quarter too."

Ed Benfield left the path, pulled down the barbwire fence, and headed among the long straight rows of Cecil Byrd's cornfield. Coming out of the cornfield, he walked through the tunnel between the stalls of Byrd's barn, stopping by the tack room to fish a jar of whiskey from the farrier box. Unscrewing the galvanized lid from the Mason jar, he took a couple of deep drinks, then replaced the jar. He kept jars hidden along every path he followed, either to drink from or to sell. "Damn niggers," he muttered. He followed the wagon path between fields, then walked north on the highway, headed toward Homer Waycaster's store.

"You all wet, Ed. What happened, been grabbling with your overhauls on?" said Bud McKinney, who was sitting on the loafers bench.

Benfield climbed the steps to the plank porch which spanned the front of the store. Waycasters's was the community social center, where the locals whiled away the hours, in the wintertime by the pot-bellied stove; in the summer, outside on the porch. It was where everyone in the cove bought everything they needed and met everyone they knew.

Bud didn't push his limits of teasing Benfield till he was sure Ed was sober enough to take it. Today, Ed saw no humor in Bud's chide. "That black son-of-a-bitch Zachariah Murphy pushed me in the creek. He's a dead nigger."

"Why'd he do that? Why'd you let him?" asked Ward Denny.

"It was that bunch of Willises, with Zachariah, and his brother and sister. I'll have my twelve-gauge next time," Benfield said. "They were down there staining the creek with their nigger piss. I run 'em off, but that moron, Zachariah shoved me off the bank into the water. Then they run like hell before I could catch 'em. I'm gonna kill the son-of-a-bitch."

Jehue Fletcher sat shirtless on the idling Alice Chalmers tractor that he had just gassed up. While listening to the men, he finished off a Coca Cola with a pack of peanuts poured in it. He hopped down, put the green bottle in the crate beside the screen door, went inside, and got his two cents bottle refund from Homer. When he climbed on the tractor, he revved up the engine, drowning out the conversation. One final glance at the group, and he nosed the tractor back down the highway toward a waiting half-mowed hayfield

Annoyed at the interruption, Bud McKinney said, "You can't just kill somebody for shoving you in the creek."

"The hell I can't!" said Benfield. He tromped into the store for his brick of Red Man chewing tobacco, slamming the screen door behind him.

"Why does he hate coloreds so much?" Ward asked. "Ain't none of them hurt him or any of his family. Why, Maudie Murphy even helped Delia when she had her children, washing clothes, cooking and all."

"Ain't just coloreds; he hates everybody. He's just a mean bastard. But I did hear that his granddaddy helped coloreds go north during the war. Maybe he's afraid folks will think he's a "nigger lover" or something if he doesn't act the way he does," said Bryce Duncan. Or maybe it's just the liquor; He don't seem so bad when he's sober, but when he's drunk he's liable to do anything to anybody. Now he'll pick a fight with a colored over nothing. Ed was half drunk, fooling around with an old pistol he bought off somebody last year when Zachariah showed up right out there in this parking lot." Bryce pointed with the pocket knife he was using to clean his greasy fingernails. "Ed said, 'Let's see if this thing works.' He started firing off shots in the gravel at Zachariah's feet, laughing the whole time, 'Let's see if you can dance like niggers is supposed to.' Zach just stood there till Ed run out of bullets in the cylinder."

"I gotta disagree. Ed's mean even when he's sober," said Ward. "He come at me once for just dropping a shovel on his foot when we was digging Luke Fletcher's grave."

"Why, Delia's come in the store more'n one time with bruises on her arms. She tries to hide it, but everybody's seen them," said Bryce. "Ain't nobody got the guts to stop him." Bryce leaned forward, hacked and spit off the porch. He looked down at his oversized dusty shoes. "Ever time Louise drags me to church, I see Delia there, same place, on the front row. I don't think them boys of hers wants to go to church, but she makes them go anyway. I guess she don't want them to turn out like Ed."

"Well, there's times a man's gotta let a woman know his ways, but Ed's a mean one. He won't give up pullin' the reins in his house. And Delia's gonna just take it cause she growed up that way. But she ain't givin' up on trying to save Ed's and her boys' souls," said Bud.

"Yeah, the Bible says a man's the head of his house," said Bryce. "No woman's gonna tell me what to do." All of the men laughed because they knew Bryce's wife, Louise. He would hop to it anytime she cut her eyes at him, and he never hung out with the men past his assigned time to be home. Bryce shrugged it off, pulled out a pack of Camels from his overall bib, tapped one out, lit it, and said through a stream of smoke, "Delia won't never leave Ed, probably scared shitless."

"Delia Benfield works hard as anybody I know," said Ward. "Edna Fletcher hired her to do housework when her babies was born. Somebody said she washes clothes for Iola Waycaster too. She's gotta work like that to make up for Ed's losing every dime he makes playing poker and drinking. If she didn't he'd lose what little's left of their farm."

"Wouldn't be that way if you assholes weren't back here behind the store ever Saturday night sopping it up and jilting him out of his money," said Bud.

Ward snapped at Bud. "Liquor don't make a man foolish like Ed Benfield, especially that old peach brandy he likes so much. I know 'cause I sample a little of my own now and then. Of course, I make the best peach in the cove." Ward bent over, cinched up his bootlaces, and tied them. "And, I can't help it if he's a sorry ass poker player when he drinks. He seems right smart in some ways, but he sure can't hide his cards or hold his liquor." Ward stood up, stretched, and began walking toward the steps. "You close down the store, Bryce, if Homer don't run you off. I gotta get home. My old woman has something waiting for me and it ain't supper."

Bud waved Ward off, flicked a cigarette butt into the gravel parking lot, rose, and went inside for another pack of Camels before heading home as well.

That night after supper at the Willis's home, Milo

and Doug sat at the table. Their mother had finished the dishes and was sewing in the bedroom while there was still light. "He's plain mean. You've seen the scar on Bob Fullwood's face. Bob didn't do nothin', just said he wouldn't come to work for Mr. Benfield no more," Doug said.

"What we gonna do? Benfield gonna kill Zachariah and maybe even us some day if we don't do something, Doug," Milo said.

"Maybe we ought to kill him before he do what they say he done to Willie Scott over in Dixon County before he move here," said Doug. "And you know what he done to Bob Fulwood up at Mr. Waycaster's store."

Sherman Willis, just home from work at the limestone quarry, overheard the boys' discussion. "You ain't killin' nobody. The first commandment in the Bible is 'Thou shalt not kill.' Me and your momma's taught you to do good and follow God's word. 'Vengeance is mine' say the Lord'. You kills a body, ain't no way out of damnation. You can't come back lookin' to be saved. Besides, white man find out you kilt another white man, you be good as dead too. Ain't no forgiveness, 'cept by God, for a black man who kills a white man. We ain't far past the time they lynch black folks, could do it again."

"But what we gonna do? You knows Mr. Benfield better than we does. He mean and he mean what he say," said Milo.

"Trust in the Lord. Pray that he protect Zachariah and all us folks. But stay away from Benfield," said Sherman. "He'll cool down." Sherman hung his hat on a nail by the door and walked out back to the woodpile, picked up his axe, and began splitting kindling for the next morning's breakfast fire. Milo and Doug sat silently for a while, listening to the axe fall. Their father usually sang some hymn to himself while working, but today only the sound of the axe on the hard oak broke the silence.

Then Doug spoke: "If Zachariah killed him, it would be self-defense cause he done threatened him, and we wouldn't be disobeying the first commandment, or Papa."

"We might get Zachariah to do it. He so simple minded, he foller us around like a hungry dog. He do anything we say."

"But they catch him, they gonna 'lectrocute him. Don't matter what Benfield did to him, "Doug said.

"Yeah, but God know it self-defense. Besides, we plan it all and tell him how to get away after he do it. He won't go to Hell even if they do catch him," said Milo. "He'll be doin' everybody a favor."

All of them stayed close to home for days until fear finally gave way to courage born of hatred. Up at sunrise, the Willis brothers walked the railroad a mile or so north to the Murphy house beside the creek. They knew that Zachariah carried water from the spring every morning. As they sat on a farm wagon under a willow tree near the Murphy's neat white home, the smell of fried pork at breakfast drifted to them on the curls of smoke that rose and washed away in the light breeze. Milo nervously tugged at the wooden brake lever as if holding the wagon back while they waited to talk with Zachariah. When he came out, the pair casually joined him, walking down the path toward the spring, well away from the Murphy house. "Zachariah, you seen anything of Mr. Benfield?" asked Doug.

"No, I be stayin' home since he say what he do."

"You can't stay home from now on. You gonna have to do something," said Milo. "Sooner or later he coming after you, or he'll catch you on your way to the spring like we done. Daddy say he heard Mr. Ed talking with Ward

Denny and some other white folks at the store, and he say he'd a killed you if he had his gun when you knocked him off of Joshua."

"You gonna have to kill him before he kill you, Zachariah," said Doug. "We'll help you get him."

"How you gonna do it? I ain't goin' nowhere near that man," said Zachariah. They stopped at the big spring under a sprawling willow just beside the slope of the railroad fill. The water rushed from a crevice in the rocks, stirring white sand into a roiling swirl that danced beneath deep clear water.

"You won't have to get close to him," said Milo. "We'll get daddy's old sixteen gauge and set you up on the cut bank beside the tracks down at Mr. Benfield's house. Then, we'll call him out, tell him we wants to make up to him, maybe work for him some. We'll ask him maybe he wants somethin' to drink. We tell him we got a fruit jar of Mr. Denny's peach brandy stashed away up the tracks in the culvert, up where Moonshine Branch runs under the railroad."

"If it don't work and he don't come out, ain't nothing lost we ain't got now," said Doug. "You watch us from up there. We'll walk beside Mr. Ed. When we steps away from him some place where you got a good aim, you shoots him."

"Why I gotta do it? Why don't you kill him your own self, Doug?"

"Cause you the one he say he gonna kill. You kill him it be self-defense. You won't be doin' no crime."

"Even the Lord won't hold killing Ed Benfield against you. You just defending yourself so you can walk around a free man like you supposed to be," said Milo.

"Well, I do be feelin' awful penned in since Mr. Ed say what he said. I don't want to stay home forever. What

Mr. Willis say about dis?" asked Zachariah.

"He say we can't kill Mr. Ed cause we ain't the ones he after right now," said Doug.

Zachariah dipped the galvanized bucket in the clear pool, watching his reflection turn to circles in the water. He let the water wash over the side and fill the bucket, hoisted it from the spring, and set it on the flat rocks beside him. He sat beside the spring a moment until his reflection stilled. He stared at himself and the red clouds in the sky and the hovering trees shimmering in the pool. "I'll do it."

§

Willie Walker had trudged up the tracks on that Sunday morning to sit high upon the railroad cut bank in Fletcher's pasture and listen to the soulful singing coming from the AME Church. Settled in the thick, pale-brown broomstraw, he pulled his knees close to his chest against the cool morning breeze blowing across the hillside. As he watched, Milo and Doug Willis walked down the tracks toward Ed Benfield's house. Willie listened to the melodious sound of "His Love Will See Me Through" as the two stopped off at Benfield's house. Milo called to Benfield, something about peach brandy. The singing and voices of praise in the distance all died beneath the sound of a passing Clinchfield coal train. After the train passed, huffing its load of empty cars onward, Benfield came out of the house. Pulling the galluses of his overalls over his shoulder, he ambled his worn path to the tracks toward the two young men. Then the trio walked up the railroad, Ed flanked on either side by Milo and Doug. In the distance, Willie listened to the *a capella* voices intoning, "Keep on watching, O ye faithful, for the time is drawing nigh. We shall see the King of glory with His angels by and by."

The view before Willie was serene. The sky was clear; the morning air had not yet begun to be seared by the summer sun. The voices rose in harmony as Doug and Milo stepped away from Benfield. The thud of a shotgun shattered the calm scene below him, and he saw Benfield bend slightly forward, grabbing his stomach. As his knees buckled, he staggered off the tracks into the weeds and collapsed. Doug and Milo ran up the tracks, disappearing in the cut below. Willie watched as Zachariah ran from the woods and lurched down the side of the cut bank, steadying his descent with the butt of a shotgun.

Hearing the blast, Delia stepped on to her porch, walked down the path, and saw her husband lying beside the railroad. She ran up the tracks, and found Ed bleeding badly, barely alive. She ran on up the railroad to Lula McKinney's house. Bursting in, she cried, "Ed's been shot!" Lula's husband, Beauford, drove them down the dusty road beside the tracks. Together, they managed to get Ed into the car and drive to the hospital in Oak Hill, where Beauford called the sheriff. By the time they got there, Ed had died.

In the heat of Sunday afternoon, the sheriff came from Oak Hill and deputized a small group of local farmers: "Ok, men, we better get going. The Willis boys said he would be in a cave just above the swimming hole on Wildcat Branch. Be careful; he might be dangerous even though he gave Milo the shotgun." Old Elihue Fletcher led the way. He knew the rough terrain, and he knew Zachariah, remembering him mostly as the little boy who brought water to the men working in the hayfields. The group made its way through the thick laurel, scrambling over the rough and rocky run of the stream to the spot below the dark mouth of the shelter cave.

The sun sat low above the cliffs of the deep cove, casting long shadows of hemlocks over the trembling glisten of Wildcat Branch running free and clear.

"Zachariah! You up there? It's Elihue Fletcher down here with the sheriff."

"Yessuh, Mr. Fletcher, I up here," returned a small voice, like an echo from the rocks above.

"You need to give yourself up, son. Come on down; Ain't nobody gonna hurt you. You ain't got no gun have you?" said Elihue.

"No, sir. I ain't got no gun. I toted it back to Milo. I be comin' on out. They ain't gonna shoot me, is they?"

"This is the sheriff, Zachariah. I promise you won't be hurt."

§

Nineteen years later, out of prison for a few weeks, Zachariah sat on the red clay bank dangling his feet into the ditch he had almost finished. He pulled off his frayed railroader's cap, wiped the glistening sweat from his lean black face, and took the green Mason water jar Billy Fletcher handed him. He was about forty but looked sixty, with his graying close-cropped hair and gaunt, weather-beaten face. Nineteen years on a road gang had taken its toll. Because of his habitual deference to any white person, he kept his cap off. The ditch was for Jehue Fletcher's new water line, now that electricity had come to Sycamore Cove. Suddenly Zachariah stopped as a tight wince crossed his face. Setting the jar beside him on the ditch bank, he clutched his stomach and coughed, spitting phlegm tinged with blood into the red clay. Billy turned away until he had recovered.

"You okay?" Billy asked.

"Yes suh, I be all right when I catches my breath and gits cooled off a bit."

He finished his water, wiped his brow again, picked up Jehue's mattock, and resumed his digging. Yet, somewhere in the back of his mind stirred a vision, a scene of clear water, of standing waist deep in the cool of Laurel Creek with his younger brother Joshua, his little sister Gertie, and the Willis brothers.

Zachariah Murphy didn't return to Jehue Fletcher's house the next day. He died a few days later. The locals said that after he was released, he drank poison whiskey made with a lead-lined radiator condenser. The coroner's report indicated that he bled to death from ulcers. They buried Zachariah in the old AME Zion cemetery in the pasture just above Jehue's house, He lies near his mother and father, his brother, and his little sister, Gertie, the cemetery's field rock headstones now grown over with pine saplings.

Ezra Murphy was gifted with the Sight. He was always predicting when a change in the weather might happen, whether the season was going to be fruitful, or when someone was coming into good fortune. He could even tell when someone might die. It wasn't surprising then that Jehue Fletcher turned to Ezra for answers to his serious questions about life, especially in his disappointing search for true love.

Jehue was the smallest and youngest of Elihue's children. He wore thick glasses, was already beginning to bald, had a large face and lopsided grin. He was quick witted and friendly, easy to like, stout but stoop shouldered. He was not tall and imposing like his brothers, was aware of that difference, and thus was not comfortable around girls. As a child he had always been a reader; even now the older brothers would laugh and joke if they caught him, "There's ole Jehue with his nose in a book!" But the teasing was affectionate, and he was the favorite of his sister Annie, who spoiled him as best she could, as if she wanted to compensate him for the lack of looks and physique that distinguished his older brothers.

He was a dreamer, a lover of music, playing the piano and guitar whenever he got the chance. He didn't have much time to practice the guitar, but he loved playing when time would allow. He had always loved being around Ezra, who had shown him chords and helped him learn a little flat top picking and bottleneck style. Ezra had always been a patient man. Now Jehue needed help of a different kind. He had been courting Matilda Gouge, who lived up north in Piney Ridge. He took her to the movies in the county seat of Oak Hill and even ate Sunday dinner with her family, a sign of rather serious intent. The courtship dragged on for nearly two years, but something just didn't feel right. It felt like they both were just pretending romance because neither of them had any other possibilities and they were expected to find suitable mates. He kept ignoring all of Matilda's hints that it was time to propose. He just couldn't bring himself to bend that knee.

He decided he had to make a decision, then thought of Ezra, gifted with the Sight, living up there on the side of Bobcat Mountain in his old shack with his family. He decided to seek Ezra's insight, to see if his vision might prove clearer than his own. As Jehue approached the shack, Ezra was standing on the porch as if he'd been expecting him. "Well, hello Jehue. Come on up here on the porch. Tell me what can ole Ezra do for you."

Jehue climbed the rickety steps and sat on the edge of the porch looking out over the valley, neither man speaking. Then he told Ezra his problem. He'd been going out with Matilda Gouge for a good spell and wanted to see whether or not he was destined to marry her.

Ezra whittled a vine-twisted maple walking stick. He didn't stop nor look up, just kept on whittling. Finally, he laid the stick down, folded up his pocket knife, and tucked it in his overalls. He didn't know, he said, but he could try to find out.

He stepped down to a little circle of rocks surrounding burnt coals and ashes, added some more twigs and sticks, and lit a fire with one of the kitchen matches he carried in his bib overalls. As he added bigger sticks from his woodpile, the flames grew. Then he announced they would need to wait till the fire burned down.

"While we's waitin' I'll fix up somethin' in the house. You can come on in if you want to." Jehue followed Ezra into the dark, crowded house. Two beds were pushed against the walls. A big oak table and four cane bottom chairs took up the center of the room. Fireplace coals glowed in the dimness, and a tall upright piano stood against the fourth wall, a banjo and guitar leaning against it.

Ezra went to a little plank cabinet in one corner, opened the door, and began removing items from the shelves—dried herbs, small bottles of brown liquids, and a variety of barks, examining and sniffing each. He placed a few broken leaves and pieces of bark in a small crockery bowl and ground them up. Then he added liquids from two bottles. Jehue didn't dare break the ceremonial silence.

He quietly followed Ezra down the porch steps to the fire pit. Ezra poked around the coals until they glowed red. Muttering unintelligible words, he poured the foul-looking concoction in a slimy string onto the coals. It sizzled and sputtered, giving off a white cloud of smoke. Ezra stood back, watching the smoke rise and drift away.

As Jehue watched, Ezra explained, "I's readin' the smoke." Then he offered his vision: "Jehue, you ain't gonna marry Miss Gouge. But I can't tell you who you are gonna marry." As he stared at the coals, Jehue waited for more. "Miss Gouge lives up to the north, but the smoke drifted south. That's where you're gonna find your woman. I can tell you that for sure."

After thanking him, Jehue walked down the holler, across the tracks, through the big field, across the highway, and back to the big white farmhouse that was his home. He emitted a little sigh of relief that Ezra had freed him from the fate of marrying Matilda Gouge. Now he remained uncertain of what awaited him. Ezra's words lingered in the back of his mind every day as his routine work on the farm continued and as he searched for a social life within Sycamore Cove.

All of the cove's social life was based on church membership and local school activities which extended to the entire community. Most of the girls Jehue had gone to school with were already married. Many in his Methodist church were either married or at least unofficially attached. He couldn't see any real likelihood of meeting a girl from the southern part of the county, where other communities were just as locked into their own social patterns as his own. Still, he wanted to believe. Months passed. Then, the following February he went by himself to the community Valentine's dance held in Sycamore Cove school.

He walked into the cafeteria where the tables had been cleared away. Staying close to the wall, he moved around the dancing couples. Small groups clustered talking, occasionally some would move out on to the dance floor. Few were alone, but he saw one pretty girl with dark-brown hair, standing by herself across the room. She wore a soft blue, flowery dress. Her eyes met Jehue's almost instantly. He glanced away, thinking that a pretty girl like her would be staring at him only because of his glasses and stooped shoulders, but when he looked her way again, she was smiling. He smiled back and walked among the dancers toward her. "My name is Jehue, would you dance with me?"

She nodded and said, "I know who you are. You're one of them Fletcher boys from Sycamore Cove, aren't you? I'm Nora Goode. My family lives down at Pleasant Ridge." She took his hand as they walked to the dance floor. "I'm visiting some of my relatives who live close," she said. "My Mama's people are from here." Jehue's faith in Ezra was affirmed, and after a respectable four months of courtship, he and Nora married in the big Methodist church in Oak Hill. Elihue, Lilian, and Annie drove into town with Jehue, while Nora was accompanied by her parents and her favorite younger sister, Mary. They were married in the pastor's study.

Most of Nora's siblings were either already gone from home or lacking in the fancy clothes they would consider appropriate for a Fletcher family wedding. Besides, their mother considered such things frivolous, although she had made Nora a nice new dress which she could use for church up at Sycamore Cove. She owed her oldest daughter that much, she thought, for being the one forced to quit school to help with the three boys who had been born so close to one another; and then the other girls coming along. It just wore her out. She would miss Nora's help, but no doubt, all that helping with the children should make her a good and obedient helpmate as was the Lord's will for all women.

But the war and all its turbulent aftermath was to bring change to valley life. Jehue joined the daily exodus with other farmers to a furniture factory in Oak Hill. Waking early to milk the cow, driving sixteen miles to the factory, coming home to more chores on his little segment of land gradually weighed upon him. The piano, which he had inherited, had been moved out of his little house and over to his brother's larger house with its separate front room, spare room, and dining room. Nora claimed there wasn't room for it in their crowded little house, and it was too noisy for the children.

He occasionally escaped Nora's stern judgement by joining the unspoken social gathering behind Homer Waycaster's store on Saturday nights. There, he could have a drink and play poker with some of the community derelicts. Among the men were tenant farmers, old men drawing meager pensions, men unable or unwilling to take steady jobs, men living in broken marriages with broken souls.

Still, Jehue held to his vision after the steady rhythm of valley life had disappeared with the sound of machines and demanding voices; the magic and music had faded away like the receding wail of the steam train engine whistles, and all that remained was the story. Long after Ezra had moved to town so that his children could finish school in this segregated county and nation, after Ezra had died and he himself was old, Jehue would tell his grown boys of the little shack where magic and music had blended. He would speak of Ezra, the man of many gifts. "I tell you boys," he'd say to his grown children. "Old Ezra had the Sight. He knew where I'd find your mother, he knew we were meant to be together, and look what happened. Here you are! Old Ezra could see things couldn't nobody else see."

Dusk had descended over Sycamore Cove. Tired farmers were settling into quiet evenings after supper. Merchants and factory workers had returned home, anticipating the weekend of catching up on chores, playing with children, and going to church. But in the woods behind Homer Waycaster's general store, darkness also brought the beginnings of comradery, tall tales, drinking, and wagering meager incomes by firelight.

"Hey, Coot, pay attention!" said Vernon. "Your bet."

"Huh?"

"Gimme that bottle and bet before I come over there and crack it over your thick skull."

"Oh…uh. See your five." Coot Rankin, a scarecrow of a man, about forty-five, was sitting on the end of an old railroad tie. He took a pull from the half empty fifth of Old Crow and passed it to Vernon. Coot was thin as a fence rail and about as weathered gray with a long wedge-shaped nose that matched his face. Every contour of his skull rippled under his taut skin, the folds matching his toothless, puckered mouth. What was left of his straw-like hair splayed in every direction. His folded knees had long since pushed through his overalls. Sighing, he threw four ones and two half dollars into the pot.

"They ain't fifteen dollars in there. You assholes are cowards. I'll see you, Vernon, and raise you five," said Basil Smoot. Everything about Basil was round: his face, his nose, his chest, his paunch of a belly hanging over his lap where he sat on a ladder-back chair frame with boards laid across the missing seat. "I'm folding," he said, throwing his cards on the ground.

A small fire burned in a circle of sooty rocks in the

center of a patch of blackened earth. The blaze gave an ancient glow, highlighting the scraggly faces of the men. Basil placed two fingers to his round lips, squirted a stream of brown tobacco juice sizzling as it hit his target in the fire, and wiped his pudgy hand on his threadbare pants.

Vernon Pate, the de facto leader of the group, took the bottle, turned it up for a quick swill, stared at his cards, and threw down his five-spot. "Call," he said. Vernon, once an imposing man, now commanded respect only within this gathering. His age was elusive, but Vernon was in better shape than the others from his earlier days of working on the railroad that crossed a dark wooden trestle just beyond the poker game. But his muscles now sagged. He had a full head of graying hair, a face that shoved forward, and heavy wooly worm brows sheltering his deep-set eyes, dark as the lumps of coal that spilled from passing trains.

"You boys got more money than sense," said Elmer Noblit. "But I'm a havin' all of it in a few minutes." Elmer, a tiny man, thin and wiry, was the oldest of the group. He was in his late seventies, but his hard life had made him look even older. His round bald head, too big for his frame, and his oversized and blocky chin suggested two different bodies somehow assembled as one. Elmer's ears stood out like the cartoon character Elmer Fudd, though his parents surely hadn't intended or foreseen the inevitable comparison other kids used to torture him during his childhood. Smiling and scratching one of his knobby ears, he said, "Okay, Vernnnonnn. Show us what you're a holdin'."

Vernon spread his cards like a casino pro. "Pair of eights and a pair of jacks lookin' at ye. Okay, old man. Lemme see you beat that." He threw another handful of sticks on the fire.

Elmer laid down a three of hearts, a three of diamonds, and a three of clubs. "They may be little like me, but three of a kind tops your fat-ass two of a kind, Vern." He reached for the pile of wadded cash from the rusting Chevy hubcap they used as a pot.

"Hold on you two," chimed in Coot. "You bastards don't never pay me no attention, pick on me all the time no matter what we're doin'. Well feast your sorry eyes on this." He threw down the two of hearts, three of spades, four of clubs, five of spades and the six of hearts. Reaching his bony fingers over the pot, he pushed Elmer's hand away, clutching at the wad of cash.

"You just wait, Coot Rankin," Vernon said. I ain't finished yet. Got my railroad pension check day afore yesterday, and I'll bet ever dime of it next week. Gonna git back at you two assholes," said Vernon. He started to get up on his wobbly legs.

"Wait jist a minute there," said Basil, reaching down and turning over each card he had thrown in.

"What you doing?" asked Coot. "You folded; you're out of this hand."

Basil turned over the six of spades, the ten of diamonds, a four of hearts, the ace of clubs and a three of hearts. "Look at that, you cheatin' old fart. Ain't never seen a deck of Bicycles with five threes. Any you fellers seen such a thing? Coot Rankin, you planted that trey. I'm takin' my money back and yours too."

"I planted it? I planted it! You drunk old buzzard. You was holdin' them threes. You snuck one of them little bastards out from up in your sleeve cause you didn't think nobody would pay any heed to little old threes. Gimme that Old Crow bottle, Vernon. I'm a gonna crack it over that fool's skull."

"Ain't lettin' go of it. It's still got a couple of swigs in it," said Vernon. "Lemme see them cards. Coot, give me the pot. I'll hold on to it while we sort this out."

"You stay out of this, Vernon," said Coot. "I ain't givin' up my winnings to nobody."

Vernon walked over to where Coot was sitting, grabbed him by the shirt collar, and jerked him to his feet. Coot's galluses fell off his bony shoulders, and his limp overalls fell to his feet. He stood there in his moth-eaten BVDs. Vernon lifted him off the ground, out of his overalls. Elmer grabbed Coot's overalls and ran around the fire pit, rifling through the pockets for the cash and stuffing it into his own pockets. "Elmer's got my money, Vernon. Look what you done now!" yelled Coot.

"Your money!" shouted Basil. "Vernon, tell that old fool to give me my money."

Vernon staggered across the dwindling fire, kicking up a shower of sparks. "Elmer, give me the pot. I'm hold-in' it till we take a look at them cards to find out which one ain't no match." He grabbed little Elmer and reached in his overall pocket.

"Watch out what you're a grabbin' in there, Vernon. Effie Lou ain't darned all the holes in my pockets," said Elmer.

"Whatever I grab that ain't money or a plug of Red Man won't be much," said Vernon. Holding the wad of bills, he stepped back across the coals, kicking up an-other rise of sparks into the night sky. "Now lemme see them cards." Coot was pulling his overalls back up and tightening the galluses. Vernon stumbled around the fire until he had gotten the cards from Coot and Basil. "Now lemme see." He took the cards to the fire pit and held them up, swaying back and forth, staring at them from several angles. "Ain't enough light to see by. Throw some-

thing on them coals, Basil."

Basil picked up a few dead limbs and tossed them on the fire. Vernon waited until the flames brightened up and began looking at the cards again. "All these damn cards are so wore out, I can't tell nothin'. Elmer, you pick up another deck afore we come back out here." He threw the whole deck into the fire, making it burn brighter in the deepening darkness.

"Why me? Why don't you git them, or Basil?" They all watched the cards curl and burn.

"Cause you're the one what gits a Social Security check regular. Nobody else can afford luxuries like cards," said Vernon.

"Cards ain't luxuries, Vern, they's important to all of us," said Coot. "All in favor of Elmer bringing new cards next Saturday, raise yore hand."

"Who appointed you president, you skinny bastard?" said Basil. He raised his hand and laughed from his round belly. Vernon and Coot both raised their hands. "Well that settles it. Thank you, Elmer, for providing us with a brand spanking new deck of Bicycles next Saturday night." They all sat back down. Vernon poked around in the fire with a stick. Basil picked up the Old Crow, took a drink, and handed it to Elmer. Lightning bugs flared, rising in synchrony in the blackness of the forest beyond the dim pool of light from the lantern and feeble fire. No one noticed them.

"You thank it's a sin, what we're a doin' out here ever Saturday night, drinkin', cussin' and carryin' on like we do?" asked Vernon. "Why, my grandmaw wouldn't even let us play Old Maids, but she'd take a little sip of whiskey and honey, even give us some when we got the croup."

"Sin?" said Basil. "I ain't right sure what that means. Everbody sins if you go by the Good Book. Don't know anybody that don't covet something, might be as simple as somebody's big old mater plants or somebody's ass. You know, like their donkey, the way the Bible says it. And, I'll have to say that I have lusted a bit for some of them women in their underwear in the Sears Roebuck catalog."

"You've done more than lusted over that catalog you keep in your outhouse," said Elmer.

"I just don't think it's a sin if a body ain't hurtin' somebody else," said Coot. "Don't know as I've hurt nobody in my life except maybe Toby Bates. When we was in the fourth grade I punched him in his nose cause he called me a nasty hillbilly. It's still crooked. You look at him next time you see him."

"I like to get out of the house and shoot the shit with you assholes about more'n anything since they fired me from the furniture plant, I guess," said Elmer.

"You call that shack you live in a house?" said Coot. "You don't have nothing to show for your years."

"You're one to talk," said Elmer. "You living with your wife's momma and daddy in a trailer on their land. Least I own my shack. Since Pearly died, I ain't beholdin' to nobody no more, do as I please. And I please to be out here on ever warm, dry Saturday night from spring till winter runs me in outta the cold. My rheumatism's got so bad I can't hardly git down to the creek to fish no more. So, what else have I gotta do?"

"We're all doing something. We're being a bunch of happy born losers. I can't fuss about that." said Vernon. "We come out here ever Saturday night and get skunk drunk. Ain't a mother's son of us going nowhere. We're all gonna wind up right where Elmer is, older'n ox yokes, poor as stray dogs. But that ain't no sin in my book."

"You better watch out old man. You're asking to be

struck by lightning," said Coot. "I been baptized, dunked completely under down yonder at the Iron Bridge when I was about eleven years old. If that preacher was tellin' the truth, I don't have to worry about going to Hell because everbody is saved that's been dunked."

"Why was you dunked?" asked Basil. "Wasn't you once a Methodist."

"Still am, you asshole. My daddy always said once a Methodist, always a Methodist. My great-great grandpa was a circuit rider, come through here and made everbody feel guilty about making whiskey. But that don't seem right. They'd been makin' good liquor here ever since they come over here on the Mayflower."

"You're a dumbass, Cooter man," said Vernon. "They didn't come over on the Mayflower. Almost everbody up in here come from Ireland, according to my daddy. They was poor as sooner dogs. You never did tell us why you was dunked."

"Preacher let us decide whether to get sprinkled or dunked. Course a bunch of younguns like us wanted to be dunked since it'd be in the swimming hole down under the Iron Bridge. At least we got purified all over, specially down on the parts that need purifying most. Sprinklin' don't get them parts," said Coot.

"Maybe we all should get dunked. Sounds like Coot's got a point," said Elmer. "I didn't even get sprinkled. Nobody in my family has been to church since the Mayflower and all them Irishmen landed at Plymouth Rock and started Thanksgiving. Ain't that where they come to? I guess that's where them Plymouth Rock chickens come from. Been thinking a lot about that stuff since I'm so old I'm about to croak."

"I had a Plymouth once before I lost my driver's license. Do we need a preacher to get dunked?" asked Basil.

"I don't think so. Ain't nowhere in the Bible that says you have to have a preacher, let alone a Baptist," said Vernon. "Now that John what baptized Jesus was probably a Baptist since he dunked Jesus."

"Well fellers, the creek right over there under the trestle is deep enough to dunk in. Let's do it. I'll baptize all of you since I've already been dunked. I'm qualified," said Coot.

"I don't know about that," said Basil. "Don't seem like it's quite right. You sure you're qualified, Coot?"

"Well, if I ain't, who have we hurt? And if I am, it might just keep us from going to Hell," said Coot. "What you got to lose?

"He's got a point," said Vernon, his broad grin emphasized in the firelight. "We just gotta get a little wet. And, by God, I think my clothes could use a good sousing in the creek anyway. Come on boys. Don't be chickenshit."

"Okay," said Elmer. "Wait a minute." He picked up the Old Crow bottle, taking a sip. They passed it around till it was nearly empty. Vernon set it back on the railroad crosstie. Coot took the kerosene lantern down from the baling wire hanger swung over a tree limb. Following a narrow path, the four of them trudged through the woods and thicket to the edge of the creek. Coot led the way with the lantern; Elmer went next to see by the light, then Basil followed. Vernon lagged behind them. Finally, they stood in a row along the bank where the slow current rippled the reflected moonlight. Coot set the lantern down on the concrete footing of the trestle, the dark crossbeams shadowing the spreading light of a gibbous moon.

"Hey, would you'ns look at that," said Vernon. "That lantern light makes the arch of the trestle look like the inside of a church. I do believe we're meant to do this."

"Who's first?" said Coot. "Elmer, you go last since you're the lightest. You don't need to stand around freezing your wet ass off while I dunk the others."

"I'll go first," said Vernon, who slogged out into the water. "Damn it's cold. Hurry up, Coot."

Coot sloshed after Vernon. "Okay, now you hold your nose while I lay you backards into the water. But first I've gotta say the words."

"Okay, just get on with it."

"I baptize you in the name of the Father, the Son, Heaven, and the Holy Ghost." Coot leaned Vernon back across his arm. The heavy-boned man's feet slipped on the slick creek rocks. He fell backwards across Coot's arm and was completely submerged, sputtering and gasping for breath as he regained his footing.

"You asshole, you just about drowned me! Get your sorry ass out of here. I've been baptized now, so I can do the otherns," said Vernon. "Come on out here, Basil."

"I ain't gonna do it. I'm fatter'n a hog. You'll drop me, and I ain't gonna drown out here in the middle of the night," said Basil.

"Okay, you wanna go to Hell? That's okay with me. I won't have to put up with your shit in Heaven when I get there," said Vernon. "Come on in, Elmer, water ain't so cold when you get used to it."

Elmer waded into the creek, taking wobbly steps as he reached for Vernon's hand. "This damn creek don't never get warm. It's dog days and still so cold its shriveling up my balls."

"You ain't got no balls at your age, Elmer!" hollered Coot.

"Okay, Elmer, let me see now," said Vernon. "Here." he said as he took Elmer by the arm. "I'm a gonna lay you backards. Hold your nose. I baptize you in the name of... uh, the Holy...shit, Coot you say it. I'll dunk him."

Coot said the words; Vernon lowered Elmer under the water, then lifted him up like a rag doll. Elmer sloshed back to the bank. "Okay, Basil, you gonna' get dunked or go to Hell?"

"I can't swim," said Basil.

"Swim? Shit, the water ain't but three foot deep!"

"I ain't coming," said Basil.

"Okay chickenshit. Let's get back to the fire. I'm freezing," said Elmer.

Vernon waded back to the bank, stepping up on the slick rocks where the others had drained on their way out. His foot slipped from under him and he fell backwards into the water, then crawled back onto the rocks.

Basil said, "You looked like a big lizard on them rocks, Vernon."

"Well, you're goin' to Hell, Basil," said Vernon, as the four made their way along the path back to the fire.

"I gotta go home and get out of these wet overalls before I die," said Elmer.

"Me too," said Coot.

"Serves you right. You assholes are crazy," said Basil.

"Crazy, maybe, but at least we ain't goin' to Hell," said Vernon, laughing. They all laughed as they huddled around the glowing coals of the fire.

"Oh, uh...Vernon, where's my money," said Coot.

"Your money?" said Basil. "Gimme my cash Vernon. I won it fair and square."

"Okay, you two bastards. I'll split it halfway betwixt you since I can't tell which one's a lyin' cheatin' scumbag. At least Coot's not going to Hell for it if he's guilty." Vernon fished around in his wet pockets. "Shit, the money's gone."

"Gone? gone! what the hell have you done with our cash, Vernon Pate? Come on Coot, let's get our money off the son of a bitch," said Basil. "Both of us can take him."

Basil lunged at Vernon while Coot undercut him around the legs. Vernon collapsed to the ground with fat Basil on top and Coot gnawing on his leg. "Stop biting me, you crazy bastard!" yelled Vernon, kicking at Coot with his free leg. Basil's weight held him down while Coot fished around in his pockets for the money. It wasn't there.

"Where's our money, Vernon?" screeched Basil.

"Gawd dammit, get your fat ass off me," said Vernon. "I don't know where the money is. Coot musta grabbed it when he dunked me. Coot Rankin, I'm gonna tear you a new asshole for bitin' me."

"I ain't got the money. If I had, why would I have bit your nasty leg?" said Coot.

"Ain't nasty, I just washed it in the creek," said Vernon, pulling his britches leg up and rubbing the tooth dents in his calf. "Least it ain't bleedin' much."

They all lay on the ground, covered in charcoal, ashes and mud. Elmer was sitting on the railroad tie, laughing and holding his hands close to the dying fire. "That cash musta floated away when I was in the water," said Vernon. "You boys want to go back out there and look for it?"

"Aw, it's floated halfway to the Iron Bridge by now. Guess we all lost this round," said Coot.

Basil picked up the Old Crow bottle and took a swig. He handed it to Coot, shook his head, picked up the lantern, and walked away along the path toward the highway. "Elmer, you better damn well bring that new deck next week," he said as he waddled away.

"I'll put out the fire," said Vernon.

Coot and Elmer wobbled along the brushy path while Vernon kicked dirt over the glowing coals. Staggering to the edge of the clearing, he reached down, flipped over a flat rock beside the path to the trestle and pocketed the wad of cash before turning to follow the receding lantern light ahead of him.

Music, drink, dancing, and idleness—the work of the devil always shadowed Nora Fletcher's very soul, the fear of straying having been ingrained there by her mother, whose Bible was well worn by constant opening, closing, reading and re-reading. As the oldest girl, Nora had early on assumed the duties of caring for the younger children—washing, cooking, cleaning, work that allowed no time for school or a social life. Dancing, according to her mother, was the Devil's way of luring young people to sin and fornication. No decent girl should subject herself to such temptations of the flesh. Men were by nature instruments of the devil and would without hesitation condemn young innocent girls to the devil just to have their own pleasure.

After years of isolation and with no marital prospects, Nora had finally dared to risk her mother's wrath. Promising to be well behaved and avoid all temptation, she found a slight crack in her mother's moral fortress and used it. Her mother's sister, who understood the situation, invited her to spend some time helping her clean her Sycamore Cove home. She could earn a little money and perhaps meet some other nice young people who, like her, hadn't married at the usual age of nineteen or twenty. At the community dance held at Sycamore Cove School, she had met Jehue Fletcher. They married, a step up for her in community hierarchy, but his family's more luxuriant lifestyle carried with it constant reminders of how far she could fall.

Jehue Fletcher had the soul of a musician. He loved listening to his older brothers as they played guitar together, old-time mountain tunes such as "Wildwood Flower," "John Henry," or "Sourwood Mountain." He also enjoyed going to Ezra Murphy's shack in the hollow to listen to flat-top guitar playing, the style Ezra's father had brought to the mountains. Piedmont Blues captivated Jehue, and he ached to play "Deep River Blues" and "Railroad Bill." Ezra showed him a few chords and fingerpicking techniques, and occasionally Jehue sneaked a little practice on his brothers' guitars. Nora's mother had labeled all of this "string music" as the work of the devil, especially the African American music and picking. Their blues singing spoke so loudly of feeling there was no denying its danger even at the safe distance she always maintained.

Later, with the death of Elihue, the division of his land, and growing post-war industrialization, the brothers all took jobs in Oak Hill, and Ray and Dave moved into town, ending their musical gatherings at the old farm. Jehue ordered a cheap Silvertone guitar from the Sears Roebuck catalog and took it to Ezra's house to learn and practice. He even began using the back of his Barlow knife to make the strings sing lonesome-sounding slides. He practiced in the evenings after returning home from his furniture factory job and after finishing milking, bringing in firewood, and working in the garden. With the fading light came his music.

Growing up, he discovered his gift for playing the piano by ear. He brought the family's upright piano to his own home, where he played big band tunes such as "Stardust" and "Blue Moon" learned from his collection of 78s. But he had a wife and two children, and the piano was loud, even with the soft pedal. Nora insisted that their babies needed peace and quiet in their small house. Eventually the piano was quietly moved back to the old home place. He could go visit his sister Annie right across the road and play it, Nora said.

After supper Jehue would steal away to the bedroom and play his guitar by himself, a restful and satisfying diversion from his many responsibilities. One evening baby Billy was lying on the bed beside Jehue as he practiced on his Silvertone, concentrating on getting his fingering right for "Railroad Bill." Billy, perhaps responding to the rhythm, squirmed to the edge of the bed and fell off with a harsh thud. He squalled out, mostly from the surprise.

Nora came running from the kitchen. She jerked Billy up, cuddled him to her breast, and gave Jehue a cold and deep stare. "You should've been paying attention instead of messing with that foolishness! What if he had fell on his head?" she asked. "He could have broke his neck." Carrying the crying Billy on her hip, she went back into the kitchen and vigorously continued cleaning the table and cabinets with one hand while calling back, "Playing around with that thing ain't getting nothin' done."

Jehue put the guitar away, went out on the dark front porch, and sat in the swing. He lit a cigarette and watched the waning red moon rise above Buckeye Mountain, staying until the blistering heat of Nora's words faded. By the time he went back inside, Nora had gone to bed with Billy asleep beside her. Jehue turned to the children's bed, sat down, and stroked Ron's head. He thought about how quickly his first child had grown from a newborn to a toddler. He undressed, easing into bed with Billy between him and Nora.

After that night he tried to play in the kitchen while Nora was working her flowers or talking with neighbors on the front porch. When they were alone, she always turned away, banging the pots and pans or turning on the radio to a gospel music station. When she did glance at him, she seldom spoke except to mutter something about wasting time and not getting things done.

As the days and weeks passed, Jehue felt the stare, the coldness, heard Nora's voice in his head: *messin' with that foolishness, could have broke his neck, nothing useful.* He had begun taking the guitar to the porch or even to the barn. But the joy of playing had left him. The guitar felt heavy, his fingers wandering the frets. The harder he tried, the harsher the sound echoing Nora's voice. Eventually picking up the Silvertone proved to be just another burden. He took it to the closet, propped it in a corner, and shut the door.

Maybe Jehue needed something to cling to, something to take him back to the days when he stood among his older brothers listening to stories of his father's early years to a time before his dreary factory job, before his own attempts at farming ceased to seem important. He kept his early life secure in his cherished stories, told and told again with new elements of exaggeration, magnified with each offering. Perhaps he needed attention, hoping the stories would gain him the status he yearned for. Or, maybe he did see that shining gold coin that he swore he saw, the one that disappeared back into the dark earth where he plowed one fall morning. For Jehue the coin was real and brought to mind the story of the Tally War of Sycamore Cove.

Such stories cling to the mountains, and the moaning whistle of the coal trains encircling Sycamore Cove was at times a reminder of the days when Camp Six, with its immigrant Italian workers who were brought in to build the railroad, was the scene of a bloody conflict. Jehue had absorbed it as he had all of the old stories.

Camp Six was set up in Elihue Fletcher's pasture at the foot of Bobcat Mountain. Italian immigrants brought to New York were immediately hauled to the Blue Ridge Mountains to begin building the railroad. They spoke little English, which worked out well for the construction company, which ceased to pay them for several months. Local company overseers ignored the workers. Finally, they refused to work without pay, chanting and marching with picks and shovels in front of the superintendent's cabin, maybe becoming somewhat destructive as neither money nor answers came.

When the sheriff was called in to arrest them, they barricaded themselves in a single shack, where they were quickly surrounded by the sheriff and the local farmers whom he'd deputized on the spot. The sheriff set fire to the shanty, forcing the workers to run. Shots were fired. Two Italians died; the others were hauled to jail. The sheriff and his men declared they'd been fired on, but nobody found any guns. The farmers took their weapons and went home. The management was later found guilty of enslaving its laborers, but after the verdict, the company just changed its name and kept on with construction. Nobody went to jail. Nobody was even fined. Most folks in the Sycamore Cove community assumed that the poor, overworked "Tallies" had just misunderstood how the system worked. After all, they couldn't even speak English when they'd come from the camp to the farms to buy milk and garden vegetables.

Jehue remembered his older brother Dave telling of the shooting and seeing the smoke, and he'd heard the story of the burial of the laborers in a cemetery on his father's land. He told it repeatedly to his boys and to his buddies, adding, of course, his own embellishments:

"My daddy let the Tallies have burying space for the two men in the black family's cemetery up in his pasture. Some of the deputies took a few of the Tallies with them to the cemetery and made them dig two graves. When they rolled one of them dead Tallies into the grave, still in his bloody, mud-covered clothes, two gold coins fell out of his pocket at their feet. Now, the folks in Sycamore Cove weren't rich at all, being farmers mostly. Temptation is strong and many a man in the valley had succumbed to it: moonshine, a little poker out behind Waycaster's store, and I'd not be surprised if they wasn't a little hanky-panky went on too. But them fellers just stood there staring at them two gold coins for the longest time. Finally, Virgil Walker said, 'Boys, I don't know about you, but I can't take no gold off a dead man. Maybe I'm just superstitious, but I ain't going to risk my soul for blood money.'"

Jehue continued, "They all stood there quiet for a while longer, looking back and forth between the man in the grave and the gold coins. Walter Honeycutt picked up the coins, clinked them together and throwed them into the grave. They rolled off the dead man into the dark earth beneath his body. The Tallies nodded at each other and started shoveling the dirt back into the grave. Them fellers didn't know a word the deputies said, but everbody there knowed what just happened. After they buried the other man, the Tallies searched around and found two big field rocks to use for headstones. Virgil Walker took his old felt hat off and held it against his chest. The others did likewise. 'Oh God, take these poor souls into thy grace. Comfort their families across the wide ocean, for they'll never know what has befallen them today. May they be returned some equal measure of that which lies with them here. Amen.' Them Tallies was Catholic, so they crossed themselves, something none of our Methodist folks ever done. Nobody said a word. The workers walked back down to the company camp. The deputized men went down the other side of the hill, back to their farms."

Plowing the field below that old graveyard at the foot of Bobcat Mountain, the sound of the coal train encircling the mountain, Jehue had come across a haunting reminder of that bloody past:

"I'm tellin' you boys, it was big as a silver dollar. Why, I could see Lady Liberty right there lookin' up. She winked at me in a flash of sunlight. Then she flipped over off the blade of that mole board plow and disappeared underground. I'm tellin' you, that thing was gold, bright as a sunflower. I yanked old Maude's reins back, but she'd done took a step or two past where I saw it. I tromped back to where it went under the turned up dirt. I got down on my hands and knees and started in rolling the sod back over. I was careful, I tell you. I dug around in there till my fingers started bleedin'. That big old gold coin was in there somewhere, I know it was, I saw it. I tell you. It's like it just vanished. Why I even went back to the house and got my shovel and rake and worked that dirt for another hour. Finally, I had to give up, but I left that part of the field alone so I'd know how to get right back to that spot later. I brought my brothers down there and had them a digging' too. They didn't believe me. They told me I was just makin' it up because of the story about them dead Tallies they buried in the old graveyard when the deputies shot them."

Jehue never stopped telling the story. Occasionally he returned to the field, poking at the dirt with a garden hoe. He was a dreamer whose hopes never materialized any more than the gold coins which he clung to even when all else was lost.

Sheriff Nub Sparks had turned his black-and-white Crown Victoria cruiser around at Buckeye Falls and was headed back down Bobcat Mountain's switchbacks. His day was about over when the radio crackled to life. "What is it, Alice? Don't tell me I gotta go back up this damn mountain. I'm ready to make a quick run by The Shack and scare the hell out of Dub and any snowbirds that might be sampling his wares," he said with a chuckle. "Then I'm home to a quiet evening of making love to myself. It's already gettin' dark."

Nub cruised with the air of a man who owns his territory. He was sheriff and would likely stay that way. An understood contract with the local moonshiners and a distribution system to deliver shine and votes on election eve assured his comfortable future. Jehue Fletcher, Wade Baucom, and other selected citizens delivered a quart of moonshine to all the outlying voters and shine connoisseurs who might otherwise not bother to drive to the polls to cast their votes. Sheriff Nub slept sound at night, his dreams untroubled by anything more than an occasional fleeting visitation of lust.

He had thought about asking Alice Smoot out, but for now he was more interested in Justine Henley. His banter with Alice was a cover-up for his plans to take Justine to the movies when he finished up this evening. "No, Nub, you can keep rolling your way, but you're gonna have to make a quick stop at Homer Waycaster's Store," said Alice. She annoyed Nub, but he was used to it. He just couldn't quite bring himself to date that tinny speaker voice.

"What could be going on at Homer's? Them old Sycamore Cove loafers out back get into it again?" Nub asked Alice.

"It ain't Saturday night, Nub. You know well as I do they won't be out there on a Tuesday."

"Well, lay it on me Alice," said Nub, taking the steep curves with practiced ease. "Glad I'm already up this way."

"Homer says somebody's trying to break into his store," said Alice. "He's staying late tonight working on his books."

"Might be a hobo. They jump slow trains once in a while on the grade up the mountain. They're usually pretty harmless, looking for a handout," Nub said, pressing the curves a little more aggressively.

Nub's experience as deputy, then High Sheriff, made him ready for almost anything. He was nicknamed Nub after his little brother had cut his middle finger off when trying to decapitate a chicken for their momma to cook for Sunday dinner. Holding up his hand like a *stop* signal, he used the missing digit to gouge anyone who pissed him off better than most who actually had a middle finger. After his failed marriage to his high school sweetheart, who couldn't take the stress of Nub's aggressive but effective behavior in his job, he lived alone, mostly in his cruiser.

Nub accelerated on the few straight stretches of highway dropping to the Cove, then slowed the cruiser, shifting into neutral and turning off the headlights, leaving only the parking lights to guide him. He spotted Spud Ollis's old black Plymouth pulled into a grassy gravel road across from the store.

Spud was a high school dropout, about seventeen years old, who worked part time at Hiram Waycaster's shade tree garage. A constant nuisance and terrible student, his departure was cause for celebration among the teachers. He was a small, bantam-like kid who had annoyed everyone with his crude jokes and loud mouth, always lying about the girls he had conquered, always bragging.

Cutting the engine and parking lights, Nub rolled his cruiser onto the roadside. He picked up his flashlight, got out of the car, hitched up his pants, and walked across the road toward the lights of the store. Seeing nothing out front, he walked into the darkness and flipped on his six-cell flashlight. Moving around to the back of the store, he saw that a section of latticework had been pulled away from the foundation. A plaid coat lay next to the hole leading into the darkness under the white frame building.

Nub shook his head, dreading what he had to do. He got down on his hands and knees and began fitting his big frame into the hole. The small creaking and popping noises he had been hearing ceased, and a weak light went out far back in the darkness. Just inside, he played the beam of his light deep among the columns of big rocks supporting the store joists.

What he saw was not what he had expected. His light beam fell on a dark, moving object with white stripes. A big, fat skunk waddled across the ground behind the rock columns, and it was headed right toward Spud, who was lying on his back under a space where boards had been pried loose overhead. He had been trying to make a hole to access the store above. Now he was lying still, hoping whoever had that bright light wouldn't see him. Nub paused a few moments to figure out what to do, then picked up a rock from the ground under the store and threw it toward the skunk, which was now waddling almost beside Spud.

Suddenly it stood up on its front legs and cut loose, aiming right at Spud and instantly turning Nub's light into a hazy fog. Spud bolted up, knocking his head against a floor joist and falling back down with a low moan. Nub could barely see the boy's wild red hair and dirty white tank top through the skunk fog and stirred-up dust. As Spud started crabbing on his hands and knees in his direction, Nub just had to watch a quick moment before backing out from under the floor. He heard Spud scrambling and clawing, snorting his way toward the hole in the lattice.

Once outside, Nub stood up, dusted himself off, and hurried back around the store. He crossed the wide porch and rapped his flashlight on Homer's locked door. Homer was crouched behind the big glass counter filled with candy, cigarettes, snuff cans, chewing tobacco, and boxes of shotgun and rifle shells. His bald head kept popping up and down beside the upright barrel of a shotgun.

"Homer! Yey Homer! It's me, Sheriff Sparks. Come on over here and unlock the door. Don't bring that blunderbuss with you. You might shoot somebody."

Homer looked up. Seeing that it was Nub, he stood up slowly, surveying the expanse of the store. Laying the shotgun on the counter, he crouched his way to the door. He was still wearing his long blood-stained butcher's apron over his white shirt, his one flourish a green bow tie. As he crouch-walked to the porch, he pulled the apron up over his nose against the smell seeping up through the floor.

"Sheriff Sparks, glad to see you! Good Lord, did you run over a skunk in the parking lot?"

"Nope, say you heard somebody breaking in? You sure you ain't been butchering skunks, all that blood on your apron?" said Nub, playing his usual game of let them worry a while. He knew Alice would get a kick out of his messing with Homer.

"I been hearing all kinds of noises under the store, especially over there under the tables holding them bolts of cloth." He pointed across the store with his free hand to the tables of cloth used by almost everybody in the valley for their homemade clothes. "I stayed behind the counter with my sixteen-gauge close by. What you reckon's going on?"

"Homer, you might want to consider not opening the store for a couple of days. Won't nobody be able to stand it in here," Nub said.

"What's happening, Nub. I ain't interested in no damn skunk right now. I wanna know who's under there! Ain't you gonna go find out?" As he walked out of the store into the night air, his words muffled by the apron, the tail lights of an old black Plymouth headed south into the darkness.

"Don't get your bowels in an uproar, Homer. Everything is under control."

"You caught him?"

"Well, you might say that," said the sheriff.

"Why're you laughing about somebody trying to break in? Got him in your patrol car, huh? Who is it?"

"Nah, I ain't got him and I don't want him. It was that worthless Spud Ollis under the store tryin' to pry some boards loose to get in," Nub said.

"Would you mind telling me what's going on?" asked Homer. "This have anything to do with the skunk?"

"Yeah," said Nub, laughing. "But it's two skunks, Spud and the one that sprayed him when I throwed a rock, a big one, right close to where that little asshole was trying to get up in the store. You shoulda seen him starting to get out from under there, banging his empty head on every other floor joist."

"You arrested him, right?" said Homer.

"Hell no. I ain't about to have that stinking little fart in my cruiser. You want him, you go get him, Homer," said Nub. "Anyways he's already gone. Had his Plymouth parked across the road. I could find him if I wanted too, just following my nose. But I ain't going after him for at least a week. And, I reckon the folks at the jail wouldn't want him right now neither."

Homer scratched his bald head and said, "I guess you've got a point, but why'd you have to throw a rock at that thing? You knowed damn good and well it would let off that stink. I don't know whether to thank you or tell everybody that comes in here to not vote for you next election."

"Don't matter, Homer. Everybody knows I've got the election covered."

"I won't be able to sell nothing for a week. And that stink will soak into everything in stock. Ain't a damn thing will take that smell out, only time, a long time."

"Couldn't help myself, Homer," said Nub. "It was just too good to pass up. After all, it was Spud Ollis we're talking about."

High Sheriff Nub Sparks left the store, got in his Crown Victoria, and headed down the valley. "Unit one to dispatch, come in Alice."

"Go ahead, Nub, glad to hear you ain't layin' somewhere bleeding to death. Emergency guys wouldn't appreciate it," said Alice.

"We're mostly good at Homer's store. But it sure was a stinking mess I had to deal with. You might want to pass a word to the deputies."

"Sure, what's that, Nub?" asked Alice.

"Just tell them, if they spot an old black Plymouth with all four windows rolled down doin' anything illegal this side of murder, don't bother trying to stop it, over and out."

S waying side-to-side to his own version of "Stardust," his favorite tune from the seventy-eight rpms he had accumulated, Jehue Fletcher sat at the Hammond Electronic Organ in Sycamore Cove Methodist Church. As he came to the end of all he could remember, he reached his calloused hand for the flat brown bottle of bourbon on the floor beside the organ bench. Unscrewing the cap, he drank just enough to keep him where he liked to be. Turning the bottle in his hand, he felt its comforting shape, all the while staring at the glowing neon cross hanging on the wall at the front of the church. It stayed perpetually lit, an invitation to anyone in need. He silently prayed for something he couldn't quite grasp.

Through his fog he played the same segment of "Stardust" again. And again. After another draw from his bottle, he staggered from the church to his old oil-dripping Chrysler 300. With nothing more than reflex control, he swerved the car the one mile back to his house, now dark.

He undressed and crawled in the bed beside his sleeping wife. Nora stirred, half awake, rolling toward him for the comfort she had felt when they were young, when Ron and Billy were still at home, when Jehu still had a good job as stock supervisor at the factory, and they had been a part of a respected Sycamore Cove family. But reality intruded when she turned toward his bourbon-laced breath. Rolling away, she threw the covers off and stood up beside the bed. This night she had had enough.

"Jehue, wher've you been? Why weren't you here for the supper I cooked you? You smell like Coot Rankin!" she said. Her voice seemed to come from someone else, someone she disliked. But her stern tone was lost; Jehue was asleep in his deep drunken void.

Unable to shake him awake, she threw the covers back over him and went into the boys' vacant room. Memory brought back past smells: baby powder, musky smell of the boys' sweat, their clean clothes just off the line, shoe polish, everything she had used to keep them looking neat. Crawling into one of the twin beds, she lay awake pondering the many ways she had tried to reach back to the real Jehue, the man she had married thirty-two years ago. Finally, the futility wearied her and she drifted off to sleep.

As usual, Jehue awoke at four o'clock. His head throbbed as he bent to pull on the stained clothes Nora would wash when she could keep him home long enough to have him change. The misery of his life also awakened with the reality of another day. Putting on his shoes and dirty socks, he went to the kitchen. But instead of stopping to start the fire in the woodstove and put the pot of coffee on as he had done for so many years, he passed through, walked out the door across the back porch, and along the short path to the Olds sitting cockeyed in the driveway. He stopped, staring, for a minute wondering who had parked it that way.

Opening the driver's door, he pulled a bottle out from under the seat. It was empty. "Goddammit," he said, throwing the bottle as far as he could into the field beside the house. Slouching into the gray-boarded garage, he opened the wooden tool box attached to the wall and pulled out a half-full bottle. Unscrewing the cap, he took a strong pull, hid the bottle in the car, and went back to the house.

Now, Jehue was in control, going about the routine so etched in him that he didn't really have to think. Starting the fire, he put on coffee and fried himself an egg and some bacon. He threw a couple of slices of bread into the greasy bacon pan for toast. He sat and ate alone at the kitchen table. Leaving the dirty dishes and picking up the milk bucket, he headed for the barn to feed and milk Foxy, their aging Guernsey. He climbed to the loft of the little two-stall barn and pushed hay down into the manger. Then, moving more hay aside, he retrieved a hidden bottle. Another drink stiffened his resistance to the day ahead.

After milking Foxy and gathering firewood, he went into the boys' bedroom and shook Nora. She awoke, having lost the will to fight. "I'm gone. I've left you some bacon and toast," he said.

Nora lay still until she heard the car crunching the gravel, the smell of bourbon and bacon pulling her down. Slowly, she shook herself awake and began her routine of breakfast, cleaning house, washing clothes, and changing the sheets and pillow cases made foul by Jehue's bourbon-laced sweat. In the afternoon she watched her soaps, *As the World Turns* and *The Edge of Night*, then went outside to that which brought her peace—flowers, sky, mountain ridges, trees. Tending her flowers, mowing and trimming her perfectly manicured yard brought her a quiet joy.

She had started mowing, but stopped when she saw Preacher Madison's car coming up her driveway. She turned off the mower and waited. He got out of the car, walked around to Nora, took off his hat, and held it in front of him, turning it nervously. "Mrs. Fletcher," he said.

"Hello, Preacher Madison," she said. "How are you?"

"Fine ma'am. I just need a word with you."

"Come on in the house. I'll fix you some tea or coffee."

He followed her through the front door, seldom used except for company. "Have a seat. What can I get you?" she said.

"Oh no ma'am, maybe a little water if you don't mind." He sat in Jehue's overstuffed chair with the hand-crocheted afghan draped across it. She took his hat and put it on a hanger beside the door.

Nora went to the kitchen, returning in a moment with a glass of water. "We have the best well water in the Cove." she bragged. "Now what can I do for you, Preacher?"

"Nora, I have to tell you something that I find difficult."

Fear swept over her face. "Has something happened to Jehue, Ron, Billy?"

"Oh! No, ma'am, I'm terribly sorry that I scared you. It's nothing like that. It has to do with Jehue, though, but he's not hurt." He picked up the glass and sipped as he bent forward, elbows on his knees, holding the glass with both hands. His eyes were cast down.

"What is it? I know Jehue's had some trouble lately."

"Yes ma'am." He looked up at her and sighed. "He's been coming up at night, playing the organ and drinking in the church. Well, the church council met and decided that he can't do that no more."

Nora stared out the picture window at the mountains, embarrassed to make eye contact. "Oh my heavens, Preacher, it just kills me to think he's been drinkin' that poison in the church when he ought to be goin' there to stop his foolishness!"

"We can't have anybody drinking in the church," Preacher Madison said. "Besides, he's causing wear and tear to the organ and leaving cigarette burns on the bench. I told him he couldn't drink and smoke in there, but he's kept on, Nora. So, against all we believe in, we're gonna lock the church every night. Can you tell him that?"

"Nowadays he's been coming home real late, missing supper. I always make him a good supper, Preacher. I thought he might be out carousing with some of his drinkin' buddies. He usually comes home drunk. It don't seem like I have a husband no more, Preacher. I've prayed and prayed for him, but it seems like God ain't listening!" Nora broke down, wringing her hands and crying, "I don't know what I've done to deserve this. I don't know what I coulda done different."

"You've not done a thing wrong. Just trust God and keep on praying. Being the good wife you are is the best thing you can do."

"I try. I've been doing just what Momma always taught me, keep a good clean house, read my Bible, and pray."

"You are a good woman, Nora. Will you pray with me now?"

"Yes, thank you, Preacher."

Pard, Jehue's collie who had been his companion since the boys had moved out, waited in the front yard beneath the silver maple for him to come home. The dog could sense the car coming before anyone could see it. When Jehue parked in the driveway, Pard greeted him with tail-wagging and face-licking joy. Jehue loved the dog.

He took one last drink and carried a new bottle to the tool box in the garage. He walked to the kitchen where Nora had fixed green beans, fried liver mush, mashed potatoes, biscuits and gravy. She didn't seem to pay Jehue much attention but methodically set his plate down on the kitchen table before fixing her own. Jehue sensed that something was different. He finished half of what Nora had put on his plate. "Don't you want any more,

Jehue?" she asked. "You look tired and like you've lost down some. I can get you something else if you want it."

"No, this is all I want. I've gotta get the chores done." He got up, picked up the milk bucket, and headed for the barn. After finishing milking and feeding Foxy, he went straight to his car without coming back in the house.

He drove to the church, pulled into the gravel parking lot, picked up his pack of Camels and his bourbon, and ambled up the walkway. He paused, tapped a cigarette to his lips, struck a match with his thumbnail, and drew a deep breath of smoke before climbing the wide concrete steps leading to the double doors. When he pressed the thumb latch on the handle, it didn't yield. After a few more tries he walked around to the side door that led to the first-floor classrooms. He found that it wouldn't open either. The church was locked. "What the hell is this?" he asked. Going back to the front, he tried to see through the frosted windows leading into the narthex. He banged his fists against the big wooden doors. Leaning forward, he pressed his head against the barrier, then turned away.

Slumping down on the top step, he unscrewed the cap on his bottle, taking a strong drink and staring across the valley at the rugged cliffs on Bobcat Mountain. Finally he arose. Almost falling, he caught himself on the handrail and swayed his way to the car. After another drink, he started the car, flicking his cigarette butt out the window. Dropping the gearshift into low, he shoved the accelerator to the floor, spinning the car around. Gravel sprayed as a cloud of dust rolled across the church yard.

"Nora, Nora!" he roared as he came into the house. He grabbed her by the shoulders. "What the Hell is going on with the church?"

Nora, afraid, feigned ignorance. "What is it?"

"They've locked the church! Have you ever heard of such a thing? Everbody's supposed to be able to get in the church. It belongs to everbody. It must be somebody accidentally locked it."

"Jehue," she confessed, "they've locked it because you've been drinking and messing up things. Preacher Madison come by here today and asked me to tell you they were locking it from now on."

"Why the hell didn't you tell me before I went traipsing up there?"

"You didn't tell me where you were going! And I was too scared to tell you," she cried. She bowed her head and sobbed, the shame of the whole day weighing in on her efforts at sustaining pride.

"Too scared, too scared! I wouldn't never hurt you, Nora. You shoulda told me, though."

"I just didn't have the heart."

"Damn them. Those sons-a-bitches treat me like this after all we've done for that pissant church. We've donated money. My daddy built most of that church hisself, him and his brothers. And they do me like this after I got the railroad to give them that fancy brass bell hanging in the steeple." He staggered as he spoke. "You remember what a big whoop-de-doo they made when they hung that bell? They had a big crowd out in front of the church. The railroad official was there. He told everbody how I come to him more than once in his office, and how I told him how much we needed a bell until he agreed. They let me speak on the steps, tell everbody how Daddy helped build the church and how much our family had give. They saw what I could get done when I set my mind to it. I hope the damn thing falls on them. I'll never set foot in that church again. You just watch. And I'll tell everbody what a bunch of assholes they are!"

As Jehue pushed away from her, Nora grabbed a kitchen chair to keep from falling, searing her arm on the stove. Jehue didn't even notice as he stormed out of the house, roaring away in the Olds. He sped up the road and pulled into the dark empty lot at Waycaster's Store. Walking around the building, he followed the familiar path through the woods to an empty clearing, muttering, "Where are they? Where'd they all go?"

Having lost all sense of day and time, Jehue stood silently at the gathering place of his drinking buddies, site of Saturday night gatherings, where they all played poker and passed the bourbon, sometimes shared a Mason jar of white liquor. He looked at the ground littered with broken bottles, decaying playing cards, crushed cigarette butts, tarnished bullet casings, and dirty candy wrappers. He sat down on a worn-slick log and slumped over his knees. Lightning bugs flashed, and katydids began singing as darkness deepened in the clearing.

Part 3

Billy in the Blue Ridge

Childhood: An Interlude

Sycamore Cove lies in one of the "Loops" of the Clinchfield Railroad, a series of switchbacks that gently descend the rugged Blue Ridge Mountains from Cedar Ridge. The steep grade was gouged to make nineteen tunnels and many deep cuts, eventually leveling out in the foothills at Oak Hill.

Once, the lonesome wail of black steam locomotives had echoed from mountain to mountain, cutting through the foggy mornings before abruptly dying as the trains entered Bobcat Tunnel behind Jehue's house. At night the hotboxes of the brakes glowed red as hundreds of wheels pressed against shining rails of the steep loop. High clouds of steam pulsed from the stacks on cold winter days as the powerful locomotives crawled up the mountains pulling a hundred empty coal hoppers back to West Virginia for another load.

Now and then one of the trains derailed, folding itself in a cut or down a fill, interrupting the slow pace of the valley. Folks would rush to pick up the free coal for their winter fires, the children always hoping for candy or toys. Sometimes a hot box would break, sending glowing steel off the tracks, catching the mountain on fire. The men of the cove would hurry to keep the fire from racing with the convecting wind up the side of the mountain.

Two spreading silver maples shaded the yard of Jehue's tiny house. The grass was thin over the shallow sprawling roots, but Billy and Ron didn't care. The shade of the trees made the hot summers more tolerable. They provided an aerial haven where the two boys played, exercising their survival skills by swinging from limb to limb, perching for hours in the highest branches strong enough to hold them, and looking down unseen (they thought) by the adults working in the mundane world below. They welcomed the invasion of thousands of ladybugs in the summer. The bright-red, black-speckled little bugs, crawling, sometimes flying, were a sign of good luck. The boys chanted, "Ladybug, ladybug, fly away home!" If she quickly flew from a fingertip, luck was theirs.

On late fall nights the boys and their cousins played by lantern light in Elihue's massive hayloft. Bins were filled with freshly pulled ears of corn. Converging in the barn, all the family men would gather to shuck corn at night, as there was other work to do in daylight hours: hog killing, plowing the fields so that freezing winter would soften the soil for spring planting, getting all the hay in for winter feed. Uncle Toad always picked on the children at the communal corn shuckings. He'd grab them and rasp, "I'm a gonna jerk a knot in your tail." They would scamper away, laughing. His sharp chin, hooked beak of a nose perched over his lip where his upper teeth were missing, and his bald head made him entertaining to the children.

He would tease them about finding red ears of corn. "If you find a red ear, that means you are gonna someday find yourself a purty brown-haired girl to marry," he'd say. Each boy secretly hoped to find the elusive red ear as he pulled dry husks from the corn. But none of them wanted the other boys to know of his interest in girls, for they all protested that girls giggled too much and were silly. Sometimes Billy helped his dad push the shucks and sweet-smelling hay through the loft holes into the mangers below. "Be careful, Billy. Don't fall through. That old bull might not like the taste of you," Jehue would laugh.

Not far from the barn stood the slatted granary,

where stored corn waited to be shucked and shelled. Beside the bins of grain stood two wooden cradles holding two large casks lying on their sides. Gathering ripe apples in the fall—Limbertwigs, Romes, Stamen, Winesaps, and a variety they simply called sweet apples—Elihue and his sons pressed them in a cider mill to yield enough juice to fill the casks. The fermenting juice first became hard cider that the children were allowed to taste and the grown-ups liked to sample often for quality. The juice then turned to vinegar which the women used for pickling, cooking and cleaning.

Sometimes the kids were allowed to turn the crank on the corn sheller that stood as high as young Billy. The boys loved to watch the machine tear the dried corn from the cobs, dropping a golden shower of kernels into a toe sack tied under the sheller. The red, naked cobs spit out the top. Lillian, their grandmother, kept a lard can with cobs soaked in kerosene behind the stove for starting the fire each morning. The family never used cobs in the outhouse, but folks did use the old Sears Roebuck catalog. To keep young minds pure, the adults quickly tore out the pages advertising women's underwear.

Two long, dusty passages flanked the sides of Elihue's barn. One protected the old McCormick horse-drawn reaper, deteriorating since Elihue had purchased the orange Allis Chalmers tractor and combine. An assortment of turning plows and vintage tools filled up the other passage. At hay baling time, the men worked the baler, the engine's *chuck-chuck-chuck-chuck-pop!-pop!-chuck-chuck-chuck-chuck*, hitting on about every fifth stroke as it passed along the windrows patterning the field. This primitive but effective system produced the tightly secured rectangular bales that eventually dotted the clean field of stubble.

The barn's tack room was a showplace for a fading way of life, the shelves holding drawing knives, curry brushes, horse and mule shoes, liniments, tonics and salves, beeswax, and saddle soap. Hanging on the walls were tarnished brass fittings and buckles, also rarely used since Elihue had bought his Allis Chalmers. Square shoe nails, nippers, and rasps filled the heavy wooden farrier's box. An ever-present, musky horse odor permeated the air.

Beneath Buckeye Mountain, the cold, clear Laurel Creek flowed sinuous behind Elihue's barn. Jehue took Ron and Billy down the path through tall raspberry canes, doghobble, and willow trees to a wide place in the river where the family bathed. Later, he showed them how to grabble bare-handed for suckers and catfish that hid under the rocks and in the crevasses between them. On good days Jehue would cut a stick to use as a stringer to take their fish home where he would clean them for Nora to fry up for supper.

When Billy was old enough to go on his own, he loved to walk to the river, which swirled a constant silver around and over mossy, rounded rocks that had traveled miles from the headwaters. He relished the spectral flash of light from trout darting about in the deeper pools.

In the winter, Elihue's barn swelled with hay. Savory salted hams, side meat, and fatback hung in the smokehouse. Lillian's cupboards were stocked with green Mason jars filled with canned beans, tomatoes, corn, pork, pickles, beets, preserves, and molasses. Floral sacks of flour weighed heavily on the pantry floor, ready for winter's baking. Lillian and her daughters cut and sewed dresses, shirts, and the tops of patchwork quilts out of sackcloth. The family slept beneath a mountain of handmade quilts on feather-stuffed mattresses.

Elihue and his brothers had built the barn with locust timbers that withstand the weathering of the years. Five generations of initials whittled into the boards of the stalls remained visible. As a child, Billy lived naively in what he knew of only as paradise, with little understanding of what made it this way. He did not know the hardships of labor and undercurrents of human frailty that weighed on the grown-ups like a heavy winter snow.

Two silver maples graced Lula McKinney's yard on Buckeye Mountain, a quarter of a mile above the course of the winding old road that clung in spots close to the edge of the mountain and dangerously crisscrossed the Clinchfield railroad several times. This was the original pioneer route that still coursed along parallel to Laurel Creek after the new paved highway had split the valley. Lula, a lanky grayed and frayed woman with a long narrow face and squinting eyes, a spry mind, and an active, high-pitched tongue, complained endlessly about the old maple roots growing across her yard. Lula spent much of her time sitting on her front porch watching and listening to the long trains carrying coal around Sycamore Cove, descending toward the power plants of the south.

Nora and Jehue often drove across the valley to visit Lula, Billy having no choice but to go along. Lula's house was only about a crow-flying half mile from Jehue's, but the complications of new and old highways and the twisting Laurel Creek quadrupled the journey's distance. Her steep dirt driveway rose up across the bumpy railroad tracks, then on up the side of Buckeye Mountain. Lulu had married into a "hollow" family, one of the families forced to farm the hilly slopes and narrow pastures sweeping down from the mountain's crest. More prosperous families such as the Fletchers had claimed the prime fields and pastures of the smooth valley floor.

Sitting on the front porch snapping green beans, she stayed put until all three were out of the car, as protocol required. In her croaking voice she called out, "Why, look who's here!"

This visit meant having to discuss the general condition of the community, politely declining the offer of food, and listening to Lulu's complaints. Her husband had been dead some thirty years. Being alone, she took any opportunity to talk, to learn any gossip that might be coursing its way through the valley. It meant hours of boredom for Billy, who was expected to stay with his mother.

"Don't get up," Nora said. "We can't stay long. Just wanted to say hello and ask about you." Billy knew *can't stay long* had no meaning at all beyond a ritual response. The family would likely be there most of the afternoon, his afternoon of play forfeited. Nora and Billy joined in snapping beans while Jehue tipped his hat and headed toward the barn for no reason but to get away.

Lula sat there on her rickety porch and surveyed the valley below, the broad fields of Sycamore Cove and the greened cliffs of Bobcat Mountain across Laurel Creek in the distance beyond the valley floor. She seemed unaware of her serene pastoral setting; she had silver maples on her mind. "I'm a gonna git Beauford to cut them things down," she barked, while pointing a bean at a big maple just beside the porch steps. "Them old roots bucks up the yard, makes it all rough. And they git in my garden too," she said.

As usual, she began reflecting on her past. "See how this house is got two doors in front," she said, pointing her crooked finger over her shoulder toward the back of the house. "It's long like this cause they built it outta two of them lumber camp shacks from up on the mountain back up yonder set side by side. Beauford and Sid drug 'em down here with a team of mules when they was still a old road up through there. It's still there, but it's all growed up now. Beauford said we'd build a better house later, but you know how men are. It ain't much of a house, but they made it tight, and it's done us fair fer all these years. I've been stuck up here ever since, havin' to grow everthing I eat, keep up a big old garden, and work my tail off canning all summer in the heat. Me and Virgil dug out that cellar—worked my fingers to the bone. They was all bloody. Why, it's a wonder I've made it."

Lula came from a line of rough men. Her father was Ned Conley, a regular consumer of moonshine. His daddy, old Jake Conley, had been known as a hardnosed son-of-a-bitch. Even his own family didn't like him. He worked them like mules and whipped them unmercifully, just for the hell of it. The Conley men had been legendary. Now Lula lived in her railroad camp shack with Beauford, her children gone. She tended her garden, surrounded by an electric fence to keep away deer, which were much easier to control than the irascible Conley men of her childhood or the man she had married.

The time passed slowly as Nora began to think about the hard life Lula lived and how much better off she was marrying into the Avery family. She thought about what a sad sight Lula's place was, built out of two old lumber camp shanties put together. She was relieved when Jehu returned from the barn.

"Nora, we'd better git going. It's about time to send Billy and Doober to fetch Foxy," Jehue said. "You know that dog will go bring that cow home by hisself most times. You take care of yourself, Lula," he said, getting in the car.

Nora kept watching Lula, standing in the yard in front of her old shack.

A tandem truck with latches and hinges on the sides of its cargo bed appeared beside the road at Homer Waycaster's General Store early one fall afternoon. The big, bold letters on the side proclaimed, "WALLY'S SIDE SHOWS, BIRMINGHAM, ALABAMA." Above and below the lettering was a cartoonish painting of a grinning gorilla lying on its back.

A medicine-man style traveler stood on an unfolded wooden platform beside the dilapidated truck, luring the boys of Sycamore Cove with his friendly booming voice. Billy and his friends watched as the man dropped the sides of his truck, revealing a large ten-by-fifteen cage. A chimpanzee about the size of a stocky eight-year old kid was crouched in one corner on the sawdust-covered floor; only his eyes shifted from boy to boy, all standing some distance from the platform.

"Now all of you stout boys come on round here up close," barked the red-faced man, waving his wide brim hat. With his scruffy dark-brown beard, he looked a little like his chimpanzee. His belly pushed his red galluses over his dirty white shirt tucked in his worn dress pants barely hid his scuffed, sharp-toed cowboy boots.

"See my little buddy here?" he asked, pointing with his thumb over his shoulder. "Ain't he cute? He likes to wrestle. We're traveling through here between shows, and I needed to stop and let him rest, give him something to eat and let him play a little before we get on our way. Come on boys, you can get closer." Warily, the three edged closer.

He paused, easing himself down to sit on the edge of the platform. The boys all stood silent as he tapped a Camel from his pack, cupped his hands around a match he struck on the sole of his boot, and lit the cigarette, drawing in a long breath. Blowing smoke rings, he squinted, the cigarette wagging at the side of his lips.

"You know what I'm gonna do? I'll let you boys in the cage to wrestle him for a dollar. If you can pin him in three minutes, I'll give you five dollars back. Look at him. He's a little feller, and you big old farm boys can have some fun with him, earn you a little cash too. How about it? I bet they ain't none of you who's ever wrestled a chimpanzee before. Just think about what you can tell everybody at school tomorrow. Who's gonna be first?"

He pointed at Roy Hollifield, the smallest. The man snapped his head back toward the cage. "Come on, boy. A young feller like you's a lot bigger'n my chimp. Why don't you go first?" Roy looked at the man, then at the chimp. Gaining his confidence, Roy stepped forward. After paying his dollar, he climbed the makeshift steps up to the cage door.

The man opened the door, Roy stepped inside. The chimp stood up on his bowed hind legs, watching as Roy moved in. As Roy edged closer, the wary animal suddenly sprang onto the side of the cage with a rasping scream. Roy flinched, looked at the other boys, then approached again. The ape leaped again, this time not stopping until it had made about seven circles around Roy before hanging by all four limbs from the roof over his head. Roy reached up and grabbed the chimp's arm, but the chimp lifted him off the floor, swinging him, tumbling, to the front of the cage. When the chimp let out a loud growling sound and bared his teeth through his muzzle, Roy backed toward the door.

"I'm not messin' with that little turd anymore," Roy said. The man opened the cage door and Roy backed out, shaking his head.

"He's a little tense from all the riding, musta needed to let off a little steam. Come on over here, Bungo!" the man said. The ape let go of the roof cage, dropped to the floor, and bounced to the man, who handed him a banana from a wrinkled paper bag. "Now Bungo, these boys are nice. They just want to play with you. You be nice, ok? Behave and play right." Walking to the back corner of the cage, the chimp sat peeling the banana, which he ate sideways.

Sensing his opportunity for glory after Roy's failure, Billy could not let the chance pass. Maybe Amy Cox would be impressed. He paid his dollar and climbed into the cage. Billy had been watching the man's method of controlling the animal. His strategy was to act like a friend, gain the chimp's trust. Talking gently, he eased forward, one slow step at a time, then reached slowly for the ape's long black fingers. Bungo's head was turned away, but he was watching out of the corner of his dark round eyes. Billy's fingers gently touched his.

The ape let out a blood-curdling scream and took the same seven laps around the cage, settling on the floor at the far end near the truck cab. Billy grabbed at him with both arms. Nothing was there. Billy attacked again but stopped cold when Bungo slammed his fist against the metal truck cab so hard the whole rig shook. Reason prevailed as Billy realized that this animal was much stronger than he seemed. He abandoned the project and his faith in animal psychology.

Jack Holtzclaw, the best athlete at Sycamore Cove School, stood feet apart, hands on his hips, laughing. The man eyed Jack and said, "Them boys just ain't got it. Bet

you ain't neither, big feller." Nobody ever dared say anything like that to Jack.

Jack slipped the white T-shirt off his muscular frame, threw it on the ground, and stepped forward. The muscles rippled in his back as he pulled himself up onto the platform without using the steps. He turned, grinning, to face the others, who hated him for his athletic prowess. Flexing his biceps, he turned to face the chimp, ducked his head through the cage door, and surveyed the battlefield.

In contrast to Billy's approach, Jack naturally sought to assert dominance over his furry ancestor. Bungo had perched himself on a triangular wooden platform in one corner of the cage. Jack lunged at the chimp, grabbing his right hand. He pulled. Bungo screamed, jerked free, and placed one foot squarely on top of Jack's head on the way to his usual seven circles of the cage before settling back on his platform. Jack, a little drunk from following the blur around the cage, lunged again. Bungo's long arms grabbed the top cage bars as he swung both feet into Jack's sweaty, muscular chest, knocking him to a sitting position in the sawdust.

After a minute or two of being bounced around every time he touched the chimp, Jack at last knew the feeling of defeat. He left the cage, this time not having to duck to get through the door. Bungo curled his lips into a grin and hurled a handful of his crap at the boys.

The man collected his money, grinned, folded up his platform, and drove away.

The heat and humidity of the dog days lay on the boys like heavy quilts. The corn was curled and dry, and even the weeds weren't growing. In the dead, damp air, the boys just tried to stay cool. Wildcat Branch, with its shade of hemlocks and maples, its late sunrises and early sunsets, offered relief from the heat when their chores were done.

It was good to be out of school.

Wildcat flowed into Laurel Creek, its famous Iron Bridge, once featured in *Post* magazine and was known locally as a good place for swimming and baptisms. Beyond the Iron Bridge, the creek slowed, dropping its sand and silt and building the wide flood plain they called The Flats. Here the water was wide and shallow, slumbering along between the grain fields and cow pastures and cradled by the dense alder, cattails and doghobble along its banks. In the warm summer, gray, thick water snakes basked on the bank and hung on the low limbs over the water. Their quick retreat into the dark, shaded water scared the boys when they were fishing. Local lore labeled the harmless snakes as cottonmouth water moccasins and anyone who thought otherwise was chancing a quick death.

Here at The Flats, warm summer nights were filled with the deep bellow of male bullfrogs competing for slender-waisted females with long but strong legs. The shallow slow current, with its dense cattails and gently sloping muddy banks, was ideal for the big frogs, which were well qualified for competition in Calaveras County and worthy of being hustled by Mack and the boys in *Cannery Row*.

It was one of those sticky summer days when doing nothing in the shade was about the only option. It was a day too hot and humid for hoeing corn, which was Billy's primary duty in the summer. It was one of those days that made the South get behind in everything. Roy Hollifield, Jack Holtzclaw, and Billy Fletcher were sitting on the rocks beside the Wildcat Branch swimming hole.

Jack got up to splash the icy water over the hot rocks, cooling them enough to sit on with his naked butt. "What are we going to do tonight? You want to go camping?" he asked no one in particular. Minutes passed as lazy as the day itself before anyone bothered to reply.

"We've been camping half the summer," said Roy. "I think we ought to do something different for a change."

Billy agreed. They'd camped above Dave Fletcher's, on top of Punch Morris Hill, in the pasture by the spring above Saul Fletcher's, and at the creek behind Wade Baucom's house. They camped simply, taking a can of Beanie Weenies or Franco-American spaghetti and some crackers. Occasionally they would take a stew pot, vegetables, a little bacon, ham or leftover chicken and throw it all together for a hunter's stew. They drank from the streams coming from the mountains around the valley. They told tales, many centering on hoped-for conquests of girls, which of course were never realized. They smoked rabbit tobacco and dry grapevines and stirred sparks from the fire with sticks, risking burning down the mountains. They slept in hammocks swung between trees or slept on the ground rolled in blankets.

"How about hunting up Cecil? He'll find something to make the night interesting," Roy said. "At least we could ride up to Cedar Ridge and hang out at the drive-in. It'll be cooler up there."

"He'll get us in trouble," Billy said. "I don't want to

131

ride with that idiot. He's liable to kill us with his crazy driving." Billy was always the cautious one, the voice of common sense, the advocate for peace.

"I'm hungry. The only thing I had for lunch was two tuna sandwiches," Roy said.

"I got an idea!" said Jack. "Let's go frog huntin' down in The Flats."

"What are we going to do with frogs if we manage to get any? We don't know how to fix frog legs," said Roy. "Besides, how are we gonna get 'em?"

"We'll figure it out," said Jack. "Besides, how do you hunt rabbits and squirrels or anything? You shoot them."

They sat on the warm rocks, quietly staring at the clear cold water.

"We'll camp out behind the Murphy's place by the big spring and cook the legs for supper," said Jack. "At least it'll make camping different for a change."

"It don't get dark till nearly nine o'clock," Billy said. "That'll make it awful late for supper."

"Aw, who cares? We don't have to go to school or anything tomorrow. As long as we get home before lunchtime my mom won't care," Roy said. "But I'll have to go by Homer's store and get me an RC Cola and a Moon Pie to hold me over if we're going to eat that late."

Roy was right. Their parents were unconcerned, giving the boys free reign to roam the hills as they pleased. The hills and hollows in the cove were no more mysterious or threatening than the rooms in their homes. Billy's and Jack's families had been in this valley for generations, and Roy's family trusted their local ancestral knowledge. They had spent more time outdoors than in, hunting squirrels and making grapevine swings on Bobcat Mountain from Murphy Hollow to Cat Face Cliffs and Dogback Mountain. They set rabbit gums in the thickets around the big grain fields and fished the length of every creek and branch big enough for trout. They picked blackberries and wild strawberries in the pastures and on the hills, walked the railroad tracks from Flint Station to Topton, and occasionally even risked running through tunnels as long as Bobcat. Occasionally they hiked to the top of Buckeye Mountain to the old ridgetop road and back. They knew no boundaries; they owned the cove.

After one more icy dip in the swimming hole to cool off before leaving the shady hollow and cool breezes, they walked to Homer's store, where they joked around a bit with the usual porch loafers.

"You know where we can get any hooch?" Jack asked Coot Rankin. Coot and some of the other men played poker and got drunk every Saturday night in the woods behind Homer's store.

"I'll get you some for ten dollars," said Coot. "I know ever bootleg joint around here." Jack waved him off as they went into the store. Roy tanked up on his RC and Moon Pie. Billy got a Coca Cola in the usual little green glass bottle, well-worn from reuse, and added a pack of peanuts. Jack busied himself with selecting ammunition for the evening's assault on frogs.

At about seven o'clock, they regrouped at Billy's house, where they had left their camping gear, then took their twenty-two rifles, hollow points, flashlights, kerosene lantern, gunny sack and headed to the creek. Crawling through the pasture fences and crossing the grain fields of The Flats, they heard thousands of spring peepers and the guttural croaking of bullfrogs in the still stretch of Laurel Creek. Darkness settled over the water. The sycamore trees, the alder bushes, and the mountains turned to black silhouettes against the deepening indigo sky. The sliver of moon coming up over Buckeye would give no light. At a favorite fishing spot, they took off their shoes and loaded their rifles. Most people gigged frogs, but the boys didn't know anything about it. Frog hunting was a new experience, but it seemed pretty basic to them, like all hunting: guns and bullets. Roy brought his shotgun.

"You can't use that thing," said Jack. "You'll splatter them all over the bank."

"They're big, listen to them!" whispered Roy. "Besides, all we want is the legs anyway."

"I'm telling you, they won't be fit to eat if you shoot them with that thing."

"It bunches good, don't spread the shot all over the cove like that old sixteen-gauge of yours," said Roy. "And I'm a good shot."

Leaving the lighted lantern hanging on a sycamore limb, they waded into the water, carrying their guns and flashlights like some combat troop on patrol, scanning the bank with lights held tight against the sides of their guns. Jack, now waist deep, was out front as usual. He was always the leader.

"Keep quiet," he said. "Shine the light right on the edge of the bank above the water. Look for their shining eyes."

They moved single file, swatting mosquitoes and peering into holes in the darkness pierced by their lights. The bottom was thick mud that had settled out of the slow-moving water. Roy had tried to wear old tennis shoes, but the mud kept sucking them off his feet. He finally threw them on the bank. The three moved silently, barely rippling the water.

Blam! Roy, trailing behind them, fired into the bank. The blast of the shotgun echoed around the mountains and died, fading into silence.

"I got one!" he cried.

"Where?" asked Billy.

Roy pointed to a mud-stained patch of water against the bank. "I don't see it," said Jack. They stared at the spots where their lights played along the bank, worked their way to the bank and searched.

Jack said, "Look at this, you dimwit. I told you so." He held up a piece of frog skin with a foot hanging from it. "You can't use that thing. We won't have anything for supper if you keep that up."

"Okay, you're right," Roy admitted. "What can I do without a gun?"

"Catch the damn things with your hands," Jack said. "Here, carry the gunny sack for us and use your light to spot the frogs."

Roy obediently took up his duties and they resumed the hunt. They worked their way up the narrowing creek, then back downstream. Now and then bright reflections would expose a big frog. Occasionally they heard the splash of a frog leaping from the bank. Billy, near the bank, was chest-deep under the overhanging limbs of a river birch when suddenly an imagined cottonmouth, really just a watersnake, dropped into the water. Billy reeled backward and sank—gun, flashlight, and all. He could hear muffled voices above the water.

"Where did he go?" said Roy. "I don't see his light. There's his hat floating downstream."

Billy floundered around, found his footing, and rose, spouting water. Gasping, he ripped the water apart like Moses to get to the lights. Clutching his gun, he held his shorted-out flashlight firm like a club to kill the monster if it attacked. Jack and Roy were laughing down the beams of light that illuminated his wide eyes.

"Get the hell out of here!" he yelled. "Cottonmouth!"

Their irksome impudence turned to sheer terror as they tore through the water, light spots flashing back and forth. Their feet dug at the muddy bank until they were safe, leaving little streams of muddy water trickling back down the bank.

Before Armageddon, Jack had shot five big bull-frogs and Billy had gotten three. Two or three were small and had been driven too deep into the mud to be found. The boys hurried back away from the bank, cramming on their shoes while scanning the ground and plowing through the bulrushes, cattails, and doghobble to get away. As they calmed down, Billy was already pondering his story for Amy Cox at church next Sunday, his brush with death, his saving them all from a deadly cottonmouth in the pitch black of night. Nothing else had worked with her. Maybe his heroism would.

Returning to Billy's house to pick up their camping gear, they first stopped to remove the frogs' legs. Using Jehue's shop workbench in the back of the car shed, Jack hung the lantern from a nail on a rafter and began skinning the frogs. He cut the bodies at the narrow waist above the legs and skinned them, sort of like pulling off rubbery pantyhose. Roy watched as Billy held the flashlight. When the legs jerked and twitched as the knife tore through the spine, there was a sudden thud. Roy had passed out.

Shining the light on Roy's pale face, Billy yelled, "Roy! Hey Roy!" Jack wiped frog blood on his wet blue jeans and said, "Let's raise his feet above his head. That's what we learned for our First Aid Merit Badge."

He grabbed Roy's feet, dragged him around to a stack of boards at the side of the shop, and propped up his feet. Blood was running down Roy's forehead from a cut he had sustained against the workbench on his drop to the floor. When he started to regain consciousness, he muttered, "Where am I?"

"You're in the shop. You passed out," said Billy.

"Oh, yeh," he muttered as his head cleared. Covered with grease and sawdust from the shop floor, he chose to sit in recovery mode until Jack finished with the frog legs. While Jack collected the bodies and skin in a paper bag, Billy packed the legs in a lard can with a chunk of ice and some fresh butter Nora had churned that morning. The boys were all wet, dirty, and not all that hungry, but they were determined to go through with the plan. After building a fire at their campsite, they stood close, occasionally turning to dry.

They lived well that warm summer night as the fire died to glowing coals. Jack rolled the frog legs in flour, frying them long and slow in a big iron skillet sizzling with butter. The legs quivered and squirmed as they fried. Jack sprinkled them with salt and pepper and threw in a little more butter. They heated leftover pinto beans from Roy's mom and browned some slices of bread in the skillet. Jack, chewing on a big leg, said, "Was it worth it?"

J ack Holtzclaw was up front, not even breaking a sweat. Roy Hollifield was dragging up the distant rear and demanding that they stop every hundred yards. He sometimes exploited the view of Lake Vance, the delicate flowers of trailing arbutus, or even the black vultures soaring on the mountain updrafts as an excuse to catch his breath. The four boys were strung out for a quarter of a mile. They labored up the steep slope just past Biddix Knob on the old unpaved and rutted road that coursed along the crest of Buckeye Mountain. They were on their twenty-mile journey required for a Boy Scout hiking merit badge.

The boys were in the throes of hormones and completely irresponsible except for completing their chores at home. Birds, flowers, or trees were of little importance to any of them except Roy, whose genuine interest had the others stopping often. Roy was not athletic, his only developed muscles being in the fingers he used for turning the pages of the likes of *War and Peace* and every other book in the somewhat skimpy collection of the Sycamore Cove School library. He constantly smiled, and a strange splay of freckles across his face under his dense shock of curly black hair was a little unsettling.

Jack was the big blond athlete, good at baseball and track, the only organized sports at Laurel Creek. As he walked effortlessly up the steep grade, he stripped off his short sleeved plaid shirt and stuffed it in his belt, revealing his tan, muscled back and shoulders. Dooley Conley was trying to keep pace behind Jack, and Billy Fletcher was struggling along behind Dooley.

Billy was stocky, blond, and farsighted. He wore

thick glasses, and his left eye focused on nothing specific across the bridge of his pudgy nose. Billy was forever relegated to the role of watcher, not player, in the status sports of basketball and baseball. He was an average boy, but methodical enough sometimes to outwit the others. He wore his brother's faded hand-me-down scout shirt with patches that showed more evidence of success in scouting than Billy had earned. When school resumed, all of the boys would be juniors except for Dooley, who would be a senior.

Dooley, a new recruit in the troop, was tall and lanky, his arms swinging gracefully at his sides as he took long strides up the steep grade. Somehow he always managed to stay clean, even while laboring up the dusty slope at twilight. Billy, trudging along behind, smiled at Dooley's appearance, his black curly hair cut bowl-shaped, his big ears standing straight out from his narrow, small head.

Every part of Dooley's being was focused on the girls who swooned all over the handsome Jack, except for those rare moments when Dooley caught their attention while playing the piano. He spent hour upon hour at the piano, fondling it, touching the keys hard then gently with his long fingers. He was extraordinary, a virtuoso performer in a community that had never heard someone who had actually taken piano lessons, who played Bach, Beethoven and Scott Joplin. Most of the local music involved male musicians fiddling, frailing, and picking around the chords of D, G, and A7, their Saturday night performances embellished by whiskey. On Sundays, men and women sang hymns banged out on out-of-tune pianos, with the exception being the fancy new electric Hammond organ at Sycamore Cove Methodist, played most effectively during altar calls.

The desolate dirt road they traveled was in one of

the most rugged parts of eastern America, a narrow hint of humanity dividing Buckeye Wilderness and the great Pisgah National Forest. Other than canteens of water, the troop had carried only lunches—peanut butter and jelly and tuna fish sandwiches—which they had wolfed down long ago.

It was afternoon. The July day was warm, and they were still on the road. The four labored toward the crest of Buckeye Mountain, where they would turn left off the poorly maintained Forest Service road and hike down the steep mountainside through the national forest into the valley below. They had started early that morning from Lake Vance, where Jack's dad had dropped them off. They had begun walking briskly along the dirt road, eventually reaching the steep slopes leading to the undulating ridge crest.

Now, hours later, they could see the broad valley floor with its patchwork of fields of wheat and corn miles below the mountain. They were still several miles away from the point near the mountaintop where they would leave the road and head down the steep slope into Sycamore Cove and the security of their homes.

"Roy, if you don't get your ass in gear, it's going to be dark out here before we get started down the mountain!" Jack exclaimed.

Roy had stopped and was sitting on a big rock, staring over the wilderness at the lake in the distance, huffing and puffing and drinking the last of the water from his official khaki-covered Boy Scout canteen. He was wearing his full Scout uniform, all perfectly matched, bought from Belk's. The others wore uniforms of unmatched parts. Jack had taken his red scout neckerchief off and tied it around his brow. Dooley wore good blue jeans and a new plaid shirt; the only evidence that he was a scout was his army surplus canteen he had hung on the red, white and blue plastic lanyard he had braided for some merit badge. All of the boys wore standard high-top, dry-ridge dusted Converse tennis shoes, except for Roy, who sported his black, hard-leather high-top, official Boy Scout shoes, which had started the morning polished to a mirror finish.

"I heard somebody say that Lake Vance has a 125-mile shoreline. It's funny that it's the same as the road number, isn't it?" Roy said.

"What? You're talking about the damn shoreline when we have to either stay out here without food and water all night or go down the mountain in the pitch dark? Come on!" said Jack.

Roy hung his canteen over his shoulder, struggled to his feet and back on to the road in his now reddish-brown official Boy Scout shoes. He polished the dust away on the back of his uniform pants' legs, restoring part of the shine. "I've got blisters the size of watermelons on both of my feet," he complained.

"Don't bust them if you can help it. They'll hurt a lot worse if you do," Dooley said.

Jack lingered long enough for Roy to catch up but started up the road before he could sit down again. The little band labored to the next crest only to see a higher one beyond the next sag in the ridge. They hurried the pace down the slope, and all but Jack painfully trudged their way toward the next crest. Jack's headband was dark with sweat, but he breathed easily. They watched the sun sink slowly behind Bobcat Mountain. Roy stopped again just before the crest, sat on a big rock beside the road, and peeled off the sock from his left foot.

"We gotta sit down a few minutes. Both of my blisters have busted."

"Sit down, my ass. The sun's already behind Bobcat," said Dooley.

"I've got a couple of Band-Aids," said Billy. "Here, put 'em over the blisters. Maybe you won't rub them so much." He pulled the frayed, wrinkled and now unsterile strips from his pocket, handing two of them to Roy. "He's got to do something to those feet, or we're not going anywhere. How do we know when to get off the road? We need to start downhill," Billy said, kicking at the rutted ridges of crusted mud left by four-wheel drive pickups and Jeeps.

Roy plastered the strips over his sores and put on his dusty shoes. "We need to go at least another mile, closer to the highest ridge. If you look up here from my house, it's about even with the highest point," said Jack.

"Another mile? It's almost dark," Roy said. "Couldn't we build a fire and maybe they will think the mountain is on fire? They always send a bunch of the men up here to put fires out. We could hitch a ride out of here."

"Idiot," said Jack. "Hunters build campfires up here all the time. You'd have to set the whole damn mountain on fire to get them up here. Then, you'd have blisters on your butt as well as on your feet."

"Stop yapping, and let's get going. We're wasting time," Dooley said.

They plodded on to the highest ridge-top, watching the western sky over the hazy Black Mountain Range in the distance glowing brilliant orange. The last of the silver linings of summer thunder clouds dimmed. Heat lightning flashed in the darkening clouds so far away that the low rumbles of thunder seemed to have no connection to the lightning. The color faded to crimson, then deep purple. The first night sounds of katydids and whippoorwills began to swell, and the dusty road ahead dimmed between the tall red oaks, sugar maples and Table Mountain pines, now just black silhouettes. The bright evening stars began to emerge between the lingering clouds. A sliver of new moon hung in the dark sky to the right of Mount Mitchell. It would give them no light.

"I can't see nothing," said Dooley. "What are we gonna do?"

"Well, if you farts would have moved on, and if you hadn't wore them hard-ass, dress-up shoes up here, we might have been down out of here by now," Jack said, grabbing Roy by the front of his shirt.

"This stuff ain't getting us anywhere," Billy said. "Are we gonna give up and stay here or are we gonna risk going down in the dark? It's rough down there."

Jack let go; Roy smoothed the front of his shirt and said, "We've gotta get out of here. My mom and dad will be worried sick if I'm not home soon."

"Aw, they won't worry. They never pay any attention to when we come home," Dooley said.

Billy agreed. "I don't think they'll worry either. We're gone all the time and camp out so much, they won't care if we get in late."

Jack dragged the rank into a sharp left turn across the roadside ditch and into the woods. It was like sinking into a black cave. "We'd better keep talking or somebody is gonna get separated. We need to stay together. I can't see nothing," Billy said.

The dry woods on the mountain top were thin and open enough for an easy pace. Jack looked up for hints of sky and patches of stars, imagining a jagged opening to follow through spaces between the trees. Then the little troop started down the steep slope of the mountain and ran headlong into an almost impossible laurel hell. They reached to touch each other as they moved single file through the blackness. Jack feigned no fear as he pulled the little troop behind him, weaving his way downhill, waving his arms like antenna in front of him to find holes in the dense brush. Each step they took was a mystery. The night was complete blackness as they stumbled their way deeper into the thick tangle. Time seemed to stop, for every struggling moment of motion forward was exactly like the last, all downward into the unknown. And then a change; they moved into an open space in the blackness and Jack suddenly lurched to a stop. Everyone closed in behind him and stood silent.

"What is it?" asked Roy, who was holding on to Jack's shirt.

Jack turned and pushed back on Roy's chest. "Stay put, look."

"What? I don't see anything." said Dooley, crowding close.

"Look in front of you, dumb-ass, stars, no trees. You can see the lights in the valley." Jack said.

Huddling on the edge of a cliff that dropped into blackness, they stared into the open space ahead. Jack had stopped just a step from oblivion. In the valley below, lights shone in the houses, and the headlights of cars crawled through the cove.

They crept along the edge of the cliff, feeling every step, clinging to saplings and laurel, moving away from the abyss until they could make their way down. The slope steepened, so they slid down on their butts and elbows, unable to hold on to each other. Dooley tripped over an ancient chestnut stump, sprawling softly on a mat of leaves, his thrashing silencing the night sounds. Billy's knees felt like worn hinges. Everyone's legs began quivering as they braked against the steepness. Then the air grew cool and moist around them. The small laurel leaves changed to the rolled rich leaves of rhododendron, and the trees turned from maples and oaks to hemlocks. They had stumbled their way into the floor of a hollow. The tall rhododendron formed a black canopy overhead.

"Is everybody here?" Jack asked.

"I'm here," Dooley replied.

Billy answered, then silence.

"Roy?" Billy asked quietly, as if he would disturb the forest if he called louder.

"Roy!" each said in turn.

There was no answer. They kept calling, louder. A reply came from the blackness, echoing around the hollow. Billy and Jack fell silent as Dooley called again. "Hey, Roy!" and Roy replied. The voice seemed to come from somewhere elusive, from nowhere. His replies grew softer until they faded away. The three remaining boys, not daring to separate, moved down the hollow among the hemlocks towering overhead, calling, stopping, listening in the silence to everything in the forest. They screamed like bobcats but could hear no more response.

An unfamiliar intensity came over Dooley. "Should we wait here and see if he can find us?" he asked.

"He was getting farther away. We better get down off this mountain and get help," said Billy.

Step by step, crawl by crawl, they fought their way through the reaching black claws of catbriers. They turned, pulling back only to find themselves in stinging tendrils and muscled arms of bark.

Billy was disoriented. He heard the forest singing, "Come deeper. Let me wrap you in my arms and keep you forever." He groped for anything familiar. They were all intruders in a hostile world, threatening and wild. This darkness was alive; it was its own order. Tears welled in Dooley's eyes as he thought of home, his piano, his mom.

Jack's confidence waned. *Downhill, keep going downhill,* he told himself.

No one spoke in the blackness. Only the crushing of leaves beneath their feet and the snapping branches held them together. Suddenly a buzz in the brush stopped them, silencing their movement.

"Rattlesnake!" yelled Jack. "Stand still."

"Where is it?" asked Dooley.

"Beside me," whispered Jack.

They stopped, stood still for what seemed an eternity. Finally, Jack gave up and said, "It's probably crawled away by now. I'm gonna move."

He stepped carefully forward in the soft leaves and pressed against the foliage ahead. The buzzing started again, right beside his ear. He carefully eased his hand up, felt along the leaves and began to laugh. "It's a jarfly," he said. He held the huge bug in his hand, listening to its buzzing attempt at freedom.

"I gotta pee," said Dooley.

Jack released the jarfly into the night. The boys relaxed enough to begin pressing downward through the hollow. The silvery trickling of water joined the chorus of night sounds. They moved farther along a little branch and worried their feet through the jumble of big rocks. Their feet hurt and their clawed skin stung with the sweat of fear and pain. The ice cold mountain water was a heart-warming guide, and the wet, moss-matted rocks were soft beneath their feet.

The hollows of Buckeye Mountain are narrow and steep walled. Rapids and waterfalls nourish deep slow swirls, giving life to brook trout, crawdads and young boys learning to swim in water so cold that it turns the skin blue, even in August. The three worked their way around massive boulders, feeling their way, soaking their

Converse shoes in the cold water. Suddenly the wet moss broke free beneath Jack's foot. He lost Dooley's grip and slid into the darkness.

"Jack!" shouted Dooley.

From the sloshing sounds in the blackness below, Jack blubbered, "I'm all right. You goofballs aren't going to believe this."

"What?" said Billy.

"I'm in the swimming hole." His splashing and the darkness absorbed his voice.

"You're a what hole?"

"I'm in our swimming hole, on Wildcat Branch."

They were safe. They had been to the swimming hole so many times that they really *could* find their way out in the dark. They knew every step by heart, every rock, every tree and bush, even every water snake along the little creek, for they spent many of their summer days making the trek to the deep pool to swim, cool, and relax from chores.

Jack, butt-bruised and soaked, swam the length of the pool and sloshed up to the flat rocks where generations had basked in the warm summer sun, picnicked, courted, and even made love. Dooley and Billy too ended their ordeal with a final baptismal exit, swimming to the other end of the pool. They crept up the rock slope like evolving amphibians and joined Jack, draining their clothes and breathing a sigh of relief. They were saved.

The trio carefully felt for their well-worn path. In the distance they heard traffic, unusual for so late in the night. "I wish Roy were with us so we could tell what time it is," Billy said.

Dooley, who needed to hear Billy's voice, answered, "What?"

"Roy, he had his Scout watch. It's got a luminous

dial."

"You think he's all right?" Dooley asked

"Little prick. If it weren't for him we'd be home watching TV now," said Jack. "He's hunkered down under a bush somewhere waitin' for daylight so everybody'll come up there and rescue him. He'll love all that attention."

"But what if something gets him." Billy said.

"There ain't nothing out here that'll get him," said Jack.

"There's bears and bobcats. My daddy even said a panther jumped over him when he was coon huntin' up on Catface one night."

"They ain't no panthers here. You know that bunch; they always take a jug of whiskey with them when they go coon hunting. Hell, they might have even seen a pink elephant," said Jack.

They stood silent for a moment. "But there are bears and bobcats here, and even preacher Henley said he thought he'd seen a panther," said Dooley.

"See," said Billy. "Even Preacher Henley said he'd seen one, and he's a Methodist. He'd never take a drink."

They hadn't had much time to think about Roy in their desperate descent. Now his voice, his face, his blisters, his uniform and his dusty black leather shoes boiled back to mind. The haggard group came out of Wildcat Hollow and crossed the open rise of Lulu McKinney's pasture. Below they could see several cars moving slowly in both directions along the old road that hugged the mountain. They walked down the hill. Immediately, car lights appeared around a curve. A '49 Ford eased to a stop beside them. It was Billy's uncle, "Toad" Clark.

Uncle Toad leaned across the seat, cranked down the window of the maroon two-door coupe, and poked

148

a flashlight beam into their worried faces. In his nasal voice he asked, "Whur you boys been? Don't you know your mommas are worried sick over you?" His round bald head glowed in the window, and they saw the usual sparkle in his prankster eyes.

"Well, what the dickens you all waitin' on? Git in."

"We're all wet and dirty," Billy said.

"Well that ain't nothin unusual, is it? You ain't got no axle grease on your butt, so git in."

"Ain't they supposed to be another'n? Who's missing? Uncle Toad asked.

"We lost Roy," Jack said.

"What you mean you lost him? He's a purty big feller to lose, ain't he?"

"We lost him somewhere on the mountain. He got separated. We heard him calling but his voice faded out. We waited and hollered for him, but we never heard him again. We couldn't look for him, it was pitch-black dark," Jack said.

Uncle Toad's voice grew serious. "Well, we better stop by his house and tell his momma and daddy, and then I'll get you young'uns home. I'll keep running the road. Maybe he'll make it out. More'n likely he hunkered down somewhere up there. We can get a bunch to head up that way in the morning."

Uncle Toad drove to Roy's house. His parents were on the porch watching the road.

"Well, I found these fellers over on the old road, near Beauford McKinney's house. You tell 'em, Jack, what happened."

Jack, his clothes still dripping, stared down at his mud-stained Converses and moved onto the bottom step. He looked like a drowned scarecrow. Words tumbled remorsefully out of his mouth. "We lost Roy somewhere up on the mountain. He got separated from us in the dark. We don't know where he is."

"Why, honey, he's in there watching television. He got home about an hour ago. He's been worried about you all. We've all been worried, setting up until we got some word."

About that time Roy appeared in the door, still in uniform except for his official black dress shoes, which were now sitting neatly polished just inside the door. He had removed his boat-shaped cap and properly folded it under his belt. "Hey, you all made it. What happened to you? You look like crap."

"Hush, Roy," Mrs. Hollifield said. "Don't use language like that. You boys want to come in and get warmed up?"

"What happened to us? How did you get here? You're supposed to be dead or something. Look at you, not a scratch!" said Jack.

"Aw, when I lost the sound of your voices, I moved back uphill a little then around the hill to the ridgeline and right into a logging road. It ran straight down the ridge and came out right behind Lula's house. The only thing I worried about was Lula's old blue tick. He came charging out at me, but the nasty old thing just jumped up on me and licked me on the mouth."

Billy turned away kicking at the gravel in the drive-way, trailed by Dooley, clutching his long arms around his shivering body. Jack turned and followed. He paused and glanced back then lowered his gaze, as he too crawled into Uncle Toad's Ford.

Bobcat Guerrillas

The weeds were coming on strong in the fields of young corn, and Billy was hard at work with his hoe. It would be his battle all summer, and he welcomed any excuse to stop a moment and look up from the endless rows—a jet contrail, a strange bird, the moaning whistle of a train, a sporty car or big truck on the highway, the taste of sweet honeysuckle nectar at the end of each row. Today, suddenly, the monotony was broken. The air around him began to pulse from the roar of overhead engines. Three giant army-green helicopters rose just over the crest of Buckeye Mountain and came toward him like angry hornets. They roared overhead, pounding the air, then began to slow down. Hovering in a tight circle, one by one they settled in the cow-cropped flat of Saul Fletcher's pasture, swinging in lazy, drooping circles as Billy watched from the cornfield. This was not supposed to happen in Sycamore Cove, North Carolina, there in the peaceful Blue Ridge Mountains in his uncle's pasture full of cow piles and blackberry briars. Yet, the copters landed near the railroad tracks at the foot of Bobcat Mountain near Jehue's house.

Sycamore Cove's history of violence was limited to fights among the poker players on Saturday nights behind Waycaster's store, a few murders, always connected with bootlegging, and an assault on a railroad construction camp. And during times of war, distant violence was apparent from the thousands of tons of military equipment—tanks, howitzers, bombs, jeeps, half-tracks, and troop transport trucks—that were carried almost daily on the trains traveling south through the cove toward

Charleston and Savannah. During World War II, Army guards had been posted at the entrance of Bobcat tunnel just behind where the helicopters landed.

During the Korean War, long convoys of troops had crawled southward through the valley on transport trucks and in jeeps. As a kid, Billy would run toward the highway when he saw them coming, stand on the side of the road, and watch the mighty army pass. Long lines of green, tarp-covered trucks and their smaller companion jeeps rolled past, the soldiers holding rifles and smoking cigarettes. All wearing the same green color, the men swung their legs from the backs of trucks and the sides of jeeps. Billy would wave in hopes that some of the men would throw him K rations: Tins of crackers, candy, something that looked a little like canned meat, cookies. He was there for every convoy, waving and carrying his booty home, stuffed in his pockets and crammed in his hands. The stuff tasted like crap but it was real Army food!

This time the green soldiers had returned, even their faces were painted green. About six of them jumped from each helicopter and scattered all directions, carrying rifles and heavy packs on their backs. They disappeared into the woods around the pasture clearing. The choppers roared back to life, lifted from the swirling grass, and throbbed their way back overhead, disappearing over the crest of Buckeye Mountain.

Billy left his corn row and ran home, where Nora was standing in the backyard holding up her apron and looking toward the pasture.

"Where'd they go?" she asked.

"Army helicopters landed in Uncle Saul's pasture! Some of the boys at school said the Special Forces were doing some practice maneuvers in Buckeye Wilderness.

I'll bet they're part of that!"

"I think your daddy said he'd heard some of the men at the factory talking, something about practice for Vietnam."

A few days later, Saul stopped by, sputtering the big Alice Chalmers to a stop beside the cornfield rows. "Billy, them soldiers are camped out in my barn loft. They seen you boys around here and said you could come over there tonight if you want to. They'll show you some army stuff."

Billy, charged with excitement, went back to assaulting the ragweed and thistles like a foreign menace. Eager to tell his buddies, he hoed with such fervor that he blistered his hands. At home, he wolfed down the supper Nora had labored over all afternoon.

"I gotta go up to Jack and Roy's. Uncle Saul said the soldiers are in his barn loft, and they said we could come over there."

"By the time you get there it'll be dark. They might shoot you."

"Mom, they're practicing."

"But if they're practicin' shooting people, they might shoot you. They have guns, I saw them"

"They said we could come. And besides, we'll yell at them before we get there and make sure they know we're coming, okay?"

"Well, be careful. You never know about a bunch of soldiers. You remember when you were little one of 'em throwed a Coke bottle at you when you was waving at a convoy down at the road, barely missed your head."

"I'm gonna take the jeep," Billy said.

Jehue had bought an old 1950 Willis Jeep panel truck, almost army green, with a puny four-cylinder engine. But it could serve as an Army truck because it was

153

bare-bones inside with two hard canvas covered seats in front with the stuffing coming out like ripe milkweed and a long stick shift in the bare metal floor. Its doors slammed metal against metal.

Jehue didn't mind the kids using it, it was a piece of junk anyway. He knew that when Billy and Ron got a little older he would have to buy a big, tough-looking car so that he would not lose status among the other dads. They would all be getting big cars for their horny sons to drive. It was a rutting phenomenon, deeply rooted in Jehue, his brothers, and all of the males in Sycamore Cove. They told legendary stories of Saul Fletcher's twelve-cylinder Packard, which he drove sixteen miles to Oak Hill in twelve minutes on the old unpaved, crooked road.

Billy jumped in the jeep, tore down the driveway, and headed north to get Roy and Jack. None of the kids ever knocked on anybody's door. Billy ran straight into Roy's house, rushing past his mom in the kitchen and into Roy's room. Roy was sprawled across the bed reading the last pages of *Moby Dick*. "Roy, you gotta put that thing down and come on," said Billy.

"Wait a minute, I've got Ahab in deep shit here. What's the rush? We're just going to hang out at the drive-in, aren't we?"

"Not tonight. I've got bigger plans. You know about the helicopters that landed behind Uncle Saul's?"

"Yeh, so what?"

"They're camped out in his barn loft."

"Helicopters are camped in your uncle's barn?"

"No, smart-ass, the men."

"What does that have to do with us?"

"They told Uncle Saul that we could come over there tonight and hang out. They're Green Berets. They are going to show us all kinds of stuff."

"Green Berets? What kind of stuff?"

"Aw, come on, what does it matter? This has got to be more fun than what we've been doing."

"Hey, I've been harpooning a giant white whale. How can you beat that?"

"Shut up and get your butt in gear. We've gotta go get Jack too."

Roy rolled off the bed, sat in the floor, and pulled his shoes on. His mom smiled and said, "Be careful." His dad was in the living room watching the only television channel received in Sycamore Cove. He didn't seem to notice the boys coming or going.

Jumping in the jeep, they forced the groaning wagon up Catface Hollow Road. Jack lived in a well-kept white house with a wide front porch near the tracks. His dad worked on the railroad. Jack was helping his dad tighten barbwire fence around their little barn lot where they kept their one heifer. The boys didn't get out of the jeep.

"Hey, Jack, come on. We've got big plans for tonight. You ain't gonna believe it."

"Don't get caught," said his dad.

Jack's dad was a burly man who had seen hard work and knocked heads with his share of other tough, heavy drinkers. He sometimes got stumbling drunk, and he had run his car off dead man's curve on Buckeye Mountain three times. Every time he tore the car into an unrecognizable tangle, he climbed up out of the hollow and walked the ten miles home unscathed. The locals said it was because really drunk people are so loose that they usually don't get hurt in wrecks that'll kill a sober person.

Billy explained the upcoming adventure as they drove back to Saul's barn. Hopping out of the jeep, they walked toward the barn in the dark, talking in their loudest voices. Twilight dwindled. The fields and trees were consumed by the deep shadows of the mountain and the pale gray of a cool full-moon night. Light glowed where the wide middle door yawned open.

"Boy, the moon sure is bright tonight!" said Roy, projecting his voice toward the barn.

"Yeh, it's cold out here too!" Billy said, with equal emphasis on volume.

"What're you idiots yelling for?" Jack said

"So they'll know we're coming."

"What difference does it make? You said they told us we could come."

"They don't know when we're coming, though. They might think we're the enemy and shoot at us if we sneak up on them." Roy said

"Enemy? What the crap are you talking about? There ain't no enemy, they're practicing. Besides, we ain't sneaking anywhere with you two. You're scaring the chickens off the roost."

"Yeh? How do you practice without an enemy? They might practice on us. What better practice than to shoot a bunch of old hillbilly kids and say it was an accident," said Roy.

The high decibel discussion continued. At the gate in front of the barn, Roy rattled the chain and latch. Then a dark silhouette appeared in the open door, backlit by the flickering orange glow from a lantern. The tall straight figure before them stood with his legs slightly apart.

Roy stopped all of the rattling of the gate chain. Now only his nerves were rattled. "He's got a rifle," he said.

"Hi, you guys. Come on up and join the party," The soldier said.

"You guys," Jack whispered. "He ain't from around here."

They melted into the barn single file through its slatted, wide-open double doors, sidling past the old gray farm wagon. They climbed up the plank ladder through the hole that accessed the second floor. The old boards creaked and groaned as they moved toward the group of men sitting on a few leftover bales of straw. Their drab uniforms blended into the surroundings, but their faces glowed in the light of their lantern. There were four of them. Colonel Cliff Greenberg, from Cincinnati, was obviously in charge. A broad-shouldered, no-neck soldier, he threw his big arm around Billy and brought the kids into the lantern light, then introduced them to Sergeant Jeff Lance, from Wilmington, who greeted them with an up-tip of his bearded chin as his deep eyes roamed. Buddy Troutman, a stiff-postured Minnesotan, ignored them. Tom Sanders, nicknamed "Tom Thumb" was a big-nosed short, stocky guy from Macon, Georgia. He threw down a card and tipped his beret without a glance their way

The boys shook hands with each of them. It felt strange, shaking hands in Saul's barn with a man called Tom Thumb and somebody from Cincinnati who had a machine gun propped on the hay bale beside him.

Billy's Great-Uncle Luke and Great-Aunt Leona had moved to Cincinnati as had many other folks from the mountains. He asked Colonel Cliff if he knew them. The Colonel laughed and said he hadn't had the pleasure.

"Two other guys are bivouacked across the pasture above the Willow Cut, manning our radio relay," Cliff said. "A good guard post." The Cut, intended as a tunnel, had collapsed during railroad construction and had gained fame because of its depth.

"You boys like some C-Rations?" Jeff asked, tossing Jack a flat army-green package. Jeff reached in a duffle bag and pulled out an assortment of packages, tossing them to the boys. The packages hadn't changed much. The cookies, tins of jam and hard biscuits were bland, but they were still Army food. They each opened their packages and ate as if they were starving, all the while looking around at the duffle bags and backpacks, radios, ammo boxes and belts, grenades, a bayonet stuck in a bale of hay, a spooled roll of blue wire, boxes labeled *explosives* in big black letters, and guns. The big machine gun leaned on the bale of hay with the bayonet stuck in it. Each man kept his own rifle nearby and had a pistol on his belt that he wore as comfortably as his unshaven beard.

Cards were spread on another bale of hay. The poker hand in front of Tom Thumb revealed two pairs, fours and eights. A few dollars lay in the middle of the cards. He picked up the cash, stuffed it in his shirt pocket, and said, "Thanks guys, later."

Buddy reached his long arm behind him, picked up his rifle, and handed it to Jack.

"Ever hold an M1, boy?"

Jack held the rifle out from his body. His eyes flashed up and down the length of the weapon. "No, never. This is an M1?"

All the boys had grown up hunting squirrels and shooting tin cans and pine cones. At Christmas, New Years, and the Fourth of July, they blasted away. They were all excellent marksmen. Billy was especially good since he had one crossed eye that looked across his nose. His brain had just learned to ignore his nose and everything else the eye looked at. Corrected by Coke bottle thick glasses, the vision in his other eye was twenty-fifteen. It looked straight down the sights of any weapon, never getting confused by another good eye. He just couldn't tell how far away the target was.

Cliff said, "You guys know why we told your uncle to

have you come up here?"

"He just said you all would show us some of your Army stuff."

"Green Berets," Cliff said. "You know why we are here?"

"We heard the Army, uh, Green Berets, were practicing maneuvers around Buckeye Wilderness," said Roy

"You heard right," said Jeff, a furrow-faced, medium built man. His buzz cut made his ears look too low. He had sergeant's stripes on his sleeve. "We're special forces that go behind enemy lines." He paced back and forth. "We're here to scope out the territory and do intelligence work, communicate back with our superiors about the position of the enemy. But that's not our primary mission. You want to know why we're here, boy?" He shot a commanding look at Roy, who stumbled back.

"Sure, but what does all this have to do with us?" Jack asked.

"You're guerrillas."

"We're what?"

"Guerrillas. We're simulating going behind enemy lines to recruit guerrillas, mostly boys about your age," He said, pacing.

"We tried to wrestle a chimpanzee when a carny man stopped up at Homer Waycaster's store once. He charged us a dollar to try and pin his chimp. The little turd beat the crap out of all of us," Roy chuckled.

"We're not talking about monkeys here kid. We're recruiting you the way we'd recruit young boys to become snipers and go on night raids on the enemy with small platoons like ours, blend in with the locals, gather intelligence," said Jeff.

"Boy, this sounds like fun," Billy said.

"Hey boy, this is serious business. And we're giving

you guys a chance to be a part of it. If you aren't going to take it seriously, you're dismissed. Get it? Right, Sergeant Lance?" said Cliff, emphasizing rank.

"Colonel Greenberg is right. We are serious about our business, but we like to have fun too. When we've accomplished our objectives, we can relax. Is there anything going on, anything to do around this god-forsaken neck of the woods?"

"Not much right close," Jack said. "But we go to Oak Hill and hang out at the drive-in to flirt with the curbhops, or go to a movie. Oh yeah, sometimes we go to the skating rink."

"We'll look into that later," said Jeff. "But it's time to get down to business."

He picked up the backpack radio, propped it up on a hay bale, cranked the handle, and held the mike to his mouth. "Delta One to Delta Two," he said.

"Delta two," crackled a voice. "What do you assholes want now? You just messed up my dream about having sex with two women in a Nash Rambler."

"Be serious, asshole. I'm trying to tell some boys about our mission."

"Mission, crap. The two of us are sitting up here on top of a damn mountain taking turn beating our meat," cracked the voice.

"Okay," Jeff said, his face growing stern. "Go ahead and jerk off all you want to, but you damn well better relay our orders to us, or you'll be on latrine duty for the rest of your hitch."

"Yeh, yeh, Sarg, Delta two out."

"Guys, I'm gonna straighten out those assholes up there in the morning. Can all of you come back tomorrow night? We need to teach you about the use and care of weapons," Jeff said.

160

"Guns?" asked Roy.

"Weapons, son. They're weapons; your life depends on them," said Jeff. "All right to dismiss the recruits, Cliff?" he asked. The Colonel sitting in the door of the barn nodded, the tip of his cigarette brightening against the darkness of the valley beyond.

The boys left the barn with their heads held high. This might gain them status with the girls, who usually just giggled when the three of them walked past.

When Billy came in the door, his mother asked, "Well, did you see the soldiers?"

"Yeh, they're gonna show us how to use weapons tomorrow night."

"I don't know. You know a lotta people's got hurt messin' with guns. You remember that Derb Ollis shot two of his toes off a while back," Nora said.

"Yeh, shot hisself with a twelve-gauge punkin ball when he was climbing through the fence with his loaded shotgun. The slug went right through his steel-toed work boot. Musta been cocked," said Jehue.

They were watching Milton Berle on TV, but Billy had gotten Jehue's attention. "Remember what I've told you about pointing guns. You already know how to use dynamite. If they have any dynamite you remember how I taught you. Them boys might be awful green about it. Be sure to punch the hole for the cap with a fresh cut stick, or you could set it off. And be sure to tie the fuse back on the dynamite. And, don't go back to it all night if it don't go off."

Jehue and his brothers used dynamite to remove stumps and rocks from the fields. He had also been known to resort to hanging sticks of dynamite in little scrub pines up on the pasture hill, rocking the whole valley with his blasts. He was a little, stoop-shouldered man who wore glasses, but he knew how to get everybody's attention.

The boys returned to the soldiers the next evening. Buddy was in charge of demonstrating how to dismantle, clean and reassemble an M1 rifle and an M1911A1 Colt 45 automatic pistol. The kids repeated every step over and over until they could do it in total darkness. Jack's perfectly coordinated hands and muscles handled the weapons with the same skill he demonstrated on the basketball court. When the other two boys, less agile, fumbled around, occasionally dropping a piece of gun, Buddy spit obscenities like bullets. "You'd be a deadass special op if you fucked up like that in real combat." Billy and Roy felt privileged to be cussed out.

The lesson continued. Tom Thumb taught them how to load and fire an M1 rifle, to communicate on a field radio, and to say "over" when finished. Finally, Sergeant Jeff said, "At ease, guys, that's enough for tonight."

Colonel Cliff came down the ladder from the loft, walking beside Billy. "What's up, Colonel Greenberg?" Billy said. His question sounded as if it came from someone else, someone from a bigger world.

"Did I see you drive up to your house in a jeep?"

"Yeh, it's my dad's."

"Two-wheel drive, four-cylinder?"

Billy's pride shriveled up. "Yeh, but it runs good."

"Well, you know that's just the kind of thing we're trying to hook up with. We'll need transportation and assistance on a couple of raids."

"Raids?"

"Yeh, we've got a mission scheduled for tomorrow night. Is there any chance you could drive?" Billy's heart pounded.

"Sure, what time? What's our mission? Can Jack and

Roy go?"

"You're guerillas, aren't you?"

Jehue had complained endlessly about his Jeep, how it had no power, how he had vowed never to buy anything but a Chevy. He had rejected the chance to buy a Ford instead of the jeep. His decision to buy the jeep was vindicated. His son was going to be driving a real Willis jeep Panel Wagon for the Green Berets.

The rows of corn seemed longer the next day and the clock moved slower. As the sun settled toward the ridge over Bobcat Tunnel, Scratcher, the half-hound dog, quit his busy nosework on the honeysuckle-covered Hog Branch bank. When he trotted home to rest beneath the big silver maple by the driveway, Billy knew supper was ready. Scratcher always waited there at five-thirty for Jehue's little jeep. Billy threw his hoe over his shoulder, picked up his shirt, and followed Scratcher. The dog's ears perked up and he rose on his haunches before the jeep even came in view. When Jehue got out, Scratcher jumped on him, his wagging tail a warm greeting. Billy stared at the jeep, which instantly transmogrified into a war wagon.

Billy ate quickly and rushed to complete his chores. He brought in the stovewood, ran to the barn to shove hay into the manger to keep Foxy satisfied, and yanked up a few bunches of ragweed along with a little lard bucket of supper leftovers for the hog in the pen beside the barn.

Dressed in a pair of old olive-green Boy Scout pants, he put on his high-top black Wolverine boots that he'd spit shined before breakfast and found the greenest shirt he had. It was plaid.

"Bye," he shouted as he slammed the screen-porch door.

Mom stood in the kitchen door holding a fresh cleaned pot and a drying cloth. "Where are you going?"

"To war!"

"Well, be careful."

Jack and Roy were waiting. Jack wore old black polyester dress pants and a tight- fittting black T shirt. His blond hair shone like a lighthouse. Roy was decked out in his full dress Boy Scout uniform: polished dress boots, canteen, cap, and leather-handled knife in a scabbard on his belt.

At dusk they pulled the jeep up to the gate. A bright full moon hung above the eastern horizon over Buckeye Mountain. The air was crisp with a late spring breeze. The soldiers came out from the barn dressed in battle fatigues and wearing their green berets. Each one carried an M-I, a 45 pistol, a large backpack, and an arsenal of grenades and ammunition belts. Their blackened faces were menacing, exciting.

"Well, men," Cliff said. "Looks like you're dressed to kill." The black grease on his slight grin glistened in the moonlight.

Roy had hopped out of the back, standing at attention beside the jeep.

"Yes, Sir!" he asserted.

Cliff turned to Billy. "You know your way around, don't you?"

"Yes, Sir. Where are we going, Sir?" Billy replied.

With a nod of his head, Cliff motioned the other soldiers toward the jeep. They obediently moved to the back. Tom Thumb grabbed Roy around his shoulder and ushered him along with them. Cliff got in the passenger's seat. He looked back at Jack, who had just slipped from the shotgun seat into the back. "Hard to see anything but

164

your head back there, boy!" Cliff laughed. "No problem though, the enemy'll just think you are the moon. Here, smear some of this on your face." He handed Jack a tin of black grease.

"Yes, Sir!" Jack took the tin and obediently became invisible in the darkness of the back of the jeep.

"Our objective will remain classified until we get there. Head south," said Cliff.

Billy drove the jeep away from the barn, past his house. Nora was still standing in the light of the doorway with a pot in her hand. Billy gave her a salute as they headed south. Soon they turned onto the side road that crossed the railroad tracks, became gravel, and undulated its way to another road bordering Lake Vance. Another gravel fork veered north and traveled the rugged crest of the mountain beside Buckeye Wilderness.

"Put her in neutral and turn off the engine," ordered Cliff. "And turn off the lights."

"Turn off the lights? It's pitch dark out there!" said Roy.

"Quiet! Slow with the brakes and coast down this hill. The moon's bright enough for us to see."

Darkness gave way to the eerie glow of the moonlit road ahead, bound between the blackness of the forest on either side.

"We remain silent from here on," said Cliff. "Stop before the curve at the bottom of the hill." A map glowed pink on his lap from the beam of a flashlight he muted with his hand. "Here," he said, grabbing Billy's arm. The other soldiers sat like dark manikins, holding their gun barrels with their clasped hands. Their eyes eventually adjusted to the dark. The area was desolate, several miles from any house.

"Why here?" whispered Jack.

"Our objective is just ahead around the bend at the bottom of this hill. You boys wait here for orders," said Cliff. "Tom Thumb, Buddy, move out; Jeff, with me." The men disappeared into the darkness of the forest beside the road, leaving the jeep doors open.

"Which way did they go?" whispered Roy

"Shhh. They said to maintain silence," Jack said

The boys sat listening to the katydids and whippoor-wills. A chorus of spring peepers filled the night from somewhere down the slope.

"I'm gettin' out." Jack eased out of the back of the jeep and crunched around to the front. Roy and Billy followed his lead. They all leaned against the front of the jeep, peering down the dim, glowing road ahead.

"Look!" Roy whispered, pointing to a black figure crossing the road from left to right at the bottom of the hill, then another and another. "It's them." They all tensed and slowly moved together down the hill, step by step, the gravel crunching beneath their feet. They stopped and stared ahead.

"What's our part in the mission?" Jack asked.

"How the crap should I know?" said Billy.

"Maybe they're scouting the target so we can all make the assault," said Jack.

"They didn't give us any guns," said Roy.

"Weapons," said Jack. They stood silent, listening and looking into the night, waiting. Roy looked at the luminous dial on his Scout watch. It had been half an hour since they left.

Suddenly, below them, past the curve in the road, a flash lit up the darkness. A thunderous explosion shook the ground followed by the rattle of automatic rifle fire tearing through the night, muzzles flashing. In the sag below, bright moonlight illuminated smoke rising from the blast.

"Oh God! Maybe we're the enemy. They're shootin' at us for practice!" cried Roy.

Billy's ears were ringing from the explosion. "Don't be silly," he said.

"Here they come!" said Jack.

The four soldiers came running fast. "In the jeep, men!" Cliff shouted.

Tearing back to the jeep, they all jumped into their assigned seats. Tom Thumb, Jeff, and Buddy shoved their way in and slammed the back door. Cliff got in the front and said, "Go!"

Billy turned the switch; the jeep coughed, started. "Which way?"

"Straight ahead and move it out!"

The jeep ground down the hill, gaining speed. "Where are we going?" said Billy.

"Recon," said Cliff.

As they rounded the curve, Cliff said, "There. Through the trees. See?"

"What is it?" asked Roy

One of the men said from the darkness, "It's our objective."

Billy saw a square lot surrounded by a chain link fence with razor wire coiled on top. Inside were big electric transformers with power lines radiating like a granddaddy spider's legs in all directions, disappearing into the night. A white sign on its locked gate read, DANGER HIGH VOLTAGE: KEEP OUT. A gray, glowing haze rose slowly in the moonlight from a black hole in front of the gate.

"Stop here!" said Cliff. "It's a power sub-station, and we just blew the hell out of it, shot all the guards and took possession of what was left for the good old US of

A. Whip her around here and let's head back to base. Mission accomplished. Good job men."

Billy drove the soldiers back to Saul's barn where they praised the boys for their calmness under pressure. They took their gear from the jeep, walked away laughing, and disappeared into the darkness. Billy turned the jeep around and headed back down the driveway to take Roy and Jack home. They rode in silence until Jack said, "What?"

"What, what?" asked Billy.

"I don't know what," Jack replied.

"It was different," Roy added.

"Aw, just shut up, Boy Scout," Jack muttered.

The boys were silent as they headed home, each one wondering, "What?"

Back home, Billy glanced through the porch screen at the little green panel truck in the driveway. Nora was waiting up. Jehue had gone to bed.

"Are you hungry?" Nora asked.

Rhoda Honeycutt had been saving herself for anyone. She daydreamed of love and buried herself in worn-out copies of *True Romance* passed from one set of desperate hands to another. At school Billy's crowd passed by her as if she were a knotty pine. Like her parents, she had few realistic hopes of climbing out of poverty and seemed destined to a hard life of working to get nowhere. She always ate in the back corner of the lunchroom and sat under the silver maple at the corner of the playground with Olive Denny, her only friend in loneliness.

Olive was short, fat, and usually smelled like fish. Billy's friends were part of the in-crowd, sons and daughters of farmers of sprawling bottomland, of railroad workers, and of merchants. Even those who worked in the local factories were grounded by inherited land ownership and family prestige. Rhoda and Olive, however, were the children of poorly paid workers who had to drive from their small hollows to work in the furniture factories and cotton mills of Oak Hill.

Rhoda was tall and thin. Her hair, which she combed constantly, was dull brown, long and stringy. Her hands were large for her frame and showed wear from hard work. Her clothes, which she made from material bought at Roses five and dime, didn't fit quite right, and nothing ever matched. She was shy and knew she was poor, making every effort to walk unnoticed on the black-oiled floors of the school or to lose herself in the magazine world of beauty, romance, and beauty-enhancement advertisements.

She was a little older than most of her classmates since she had repeated the second and fourth grades. Often, she missed school to take care of younger brothers and sisters. Sometimes she returned with bruises on her arms and face. Her father was a binge drinker who would disappear for a few weeks each year, then show up sober, begging for forgiveness, which her mother always granted. He habitually got fired, moving from factory to factory, drinking up and gambling away what little money the family had scraped together. Rhoda had been taught by her mother that a good woman agrees to take her man to be her lawfully wedded husband, no matter how much of a son-of-a-bitch he is or becomes, so help her God. Her mother loyally attended church, testifying that tolerance and faithfulness would someday cure her husband's intemperance. She earned a little money working at home pairing socks for the local hosiery mill, which still paid for home piecework.

Rhoda yearned to get away from her life. The family lived in a hollow, in a typical little rectangular house with grayed lap siding. If it hadn't been so poorly kept, the house, with its little front porch stoop supported by drunken-seeming stacks of flat rocks, would have been considered quaint by summer tourists. It sat alone at the end of a half-mile dirt driveway at the head of Bobcat Creek near the railroad track. It was surrounded by hulks of dead cars, a little patch of land, and a lean-to barn. The family had a cow and a few chickens.

Billy drove bus number twenty-eight on Rhoda's route. Bobcat Creek Road ended abruptly at her driveway, where Billy picked up Rebecca, Ruth, Roman, and Rhoda, the ones old enough to go to school.

About halfway up the steep switchback road, he picked up Jake Bartlett, a tall, lanky boy about Rhoda's age. Jake, like most of the boys, had to ride the bus. Sycamore Cove fathers drove the family cars to nearby factories. The bus rides provided daily social initiation, including the frequent fights among rutting boys.

Jake's hair was as black as the grease ground into his knuckles and fingernails. His face was long and narrow and his head blended into his neck about as well as that of a chicken. With his wide set eyes and his beaklike nose, he looked as if he were always going forward, even leaning his long body into his walk. His grease-stained jeans and worn plaid shirts hung loose on his lean frame.

Jake helped his father restore brief lives to cars that by all rights should have been laid to rest in a junkyard. As with Frankenstein's monster, the cars they fixed were stitched together assemblages of the dead. And as with the monster, they were dangerous and unpredictable.

Jake talked about moving to Detroit and spent most of his time arched over his desk in the back of the classroom near Rhoda, drawing sleek cars with huge sweptback fins. He seldom smiled or turned his head, only cutting his eyes occasionally in the hall when Rhoda raised her head from a passionate scene in *True Romance* and gave him a glance. Those interactions became more frequent, their desks creeping closer together each day. Jake passed Rhoda pictures of big cars with long, pointed hood ornaments, two bulging headlights and high rounded fins. She blushed and quickly handed them back to him across the narrowing aisle.

They began sitting together in the lunchroom, seldom looking at each other at first, then wallowing in each other's gazes. At recess each day they began disappearing. Poor little Olive looked like a lonely Buddha squatted under the silver maple.

The school ground was beside the creek, which was

hidden by about a hundred yards of doghobble, alder, peeling sycamores and river birch. Little paths formed a maze in the bushes and trees where years of school kids had dared to venture beyond the playground boundary, the mowed grass behind the baseball field's chicken-wire backstop. Called by bodily needs or by boredom, they had created little trails of defiance.

The cold winter had passed, and the first lush green of the valley promised a new season of baby birds, new calves and bare feet. Flowers burst from their buds, and honeybees moved with purpose over locust flowers, yellow poplar, and clover. Baseball season was beginning, and Billy Avery, the team manager who took care of the equipment and kept score, a job that would make him eligible for a coveted letter for his jacket, was on the field. He'd finished his greasy lunch of green beans overcooked in fatback, mashed potatoes, and fried livermush. The call of nature pulled Billy's attention away from laying out the lime-white baseball diamond. He took the path into the thicket toward the creek. Moving into the woods toward a properly obscure place behind a patch of doghobble, he heard what he thought was an injured animal, maybe a hawk making its kill. High squeals, low moans, and the thrashing of leaves said something was bigger than a rabbit. As he stepped around the thick foliage toward the sound, a skinny, pale butt rose and fell above the low bush leaves. Jake's pointed face pressed into one of Rhoda's small round breasts nuzzled by his beak from beneath her stiff wired and heavily padded bra. Her cotton print dress, unbuttoned to the waist and pulled up, was wrapped like a rope around her bony hips. Jake's ankles argued with each other as he tried to get his jeans over his brogans. Rhoda's panties clung to her ankle, wrapped around his waist. He heaved his thin arch

173

of a frame above her, moving with amazing speed and rhythm.

"More, come on Jake, deeper, harder, push!" Rhoda squealed. She arched her head back into the purple sweater she used for a pillow. Never having seen the sex act before, Billy crouched in silence and wonder.

"Oh, oh, oh," Jake was muttering in rhythm with his body. He moved faster and faster as he shoved himself forward on Rhoda's pale curves. Suddenly, she raised her legs toward heaven on either side of him, waving her panties like a white flag. Making grunting sounds, he turned beet red and collapsed on top of her, her leg fell limp. They lay still, both heaving deep breaths of the spring air.

"I love you. I love you, Jake," Rhoda panted into Jake's oversized ear.

Jake said nothing. Billy eased his way back toward the baseball field. Any sound had been covered by their pounding hearts and wheezing breath. Billy's call of nature could wait. Jack Holtzclaw had just finished his practice pitches and was ambling back toward the building, tossing the ball into the air. Billy caught up with him.

"They were doin' it," he said to Jack.

"Who was doin' what?"

"Rhoda and Jake, in the woods by the creek."

"What the hell are you talking about?"

"Rhoda and Jake; they were screwing in the woods. I saw them."

Jack stopped. "You're joking, right?"

"No, they were doin' it right there behind the bushes, not far from the creek. He was on top of her. You watch, they'll come out in a few minutes before recess is over." They sat on the school steps at the back door, watching.

Jack kept throwing the ball in the air.

"Well, what have we got here? There's half the truth of your story," said Jack.

Rhoda, smoothing down her dress, was easing out of the woods well beyond third base into left field. The boys crouched and looked over the top column of the steps. Rhoda paused, glanced around, and ran quickly among the red oaks shading the perimeter of the playground. Making her way toward the building, she disappeared around the corner, heading to the other school door. Jake came ambling out of the woods behind the backstop, hands in his pockets, kicking the dirt and whistling through his tubular lips. Looking nonchalant, he weaved his way back toward the steps where Jack and Billy intentionally sat in his way. Jake stopped momentarily to survey a way around them.

"Whatchee doing, Jake?" asked Jack.

"Aw, nothing, just took a good old country dump in the thicket."

"You better watch out. Mr. Mitchell will make you write on the blackboard a hundred times, that you've been messin' around in the woods. They say he knows everything that goes on down there anyway," Jack said, as he slipped aside a little. Jake looked nervous, not replying as he went inside.

The lovers occasionally continued their ventures throughout the spring. Sometimes the boys took turns watching. Everyone knew of their frolics. Finally, it seemed as if just knowing wasn't enough. Yet, no one would tell, not even Sarah Cox, who went to Deep Cove Free Will Baptist.

"I'm gonna' fix 'em," said Cecil Pentland. "They shouldn't have all that fun without paying for it." Cecil didn't like Jake. They were both near the academic

175

bottom of the class, but Cecil was coarse and irreverent, always getting his way through intimidation, while Jake was shy and withdrawn. Cecil was ruddy and blond, lean and muscular from working in his dad's apple orchard. He had his own car, a big, powerful red-and-white Olds 88 coupe, the envy of every other boy. Wherever he was, life was interesting.

"You'll get them caught and get yourself into it too if you go down there causing some kind of ruckus," Roy said.

"You just watch me. I'm gonna make that bean-pole's little pecker shrivel up, and Rhoda pee all over herself and him too, the little slut."

"Whatever it is, you're doin' it by yourself."

Jack said, "If you're going down there, we'll stay on the field and look out for you. I'll whistle if anybody heads that way." He let loose a shrill whistle by tightly tucking his lips inward. "Even a hollow head like you can hear that, can't you?"

A few days later, Cecil followed Rhoda and Jake into the woods, staying just far enough behind. Well concealed by the thicket, he waited until they were improperly entangled before rushing toward them through the doghobble, yelling.

"Git, git out of here dog! You don't come a growling at me like that!" he shouted. "Git on, heah. If I git a holt of you I'll beat you're head into a pulp! I'll bring my shotgun down here and fill your ass full of buckshot if you ever bare your teeth at me like that again!"

Rolling off Rhoda, Jake jumped to his feet, pulling his underwear and britches half way up. He thrashed away toward the creek, his bare butt bouncing, wobbling and glowing in the dark, dense foliage. Rhoda lay panicky on the ground, reaching desperately for her panties with one hand as she pulled at her bra and dress with the other, trying to reassemble herself.

Cecil parked himself against a leaning sycamore and said, "Why, hi Rhoda. It's a little cool to be dressed that way, ain't it?" Something splashed in the distance.

Rhoda was groping for her shoes and tugging at her clothes.

"A little," she said.

"Did you see that dog go by here? Why, I thought that thing was gonna tear me apart over there where I was trying to do my business." Cecil pointed in some vague direction, then calmly walked back toward the baseball field, broke into the open, and strolled past Jack, Roy and Billy without saying a word. They ran after him, pulling at his shirt and arms.

Rhoda had pulled herself up, straightened her clothes, brushed away a little of the evidence, and followed Cecil's path straight back into the open grass and blue sky. She stood momentarily on home plate, then walked a straight line across the pitcher's mound and second base, through center field and up the steps, slamming the door behind her.

Jake and Rhoda did not return to school in the fall. They got married at Sycamore Cove Methodist in July and moved into a trailer beside the creek just upstream from Jake's dad's garage. Jack, Roy, and Billy went to the wedding since everybody usually attended all church functions at Sycamore Cove Methodist: weddings, funerals, reunions, Bible school, Methodist Youth Fellowship and Boy Scout meetings.

Preacher Henley conducted the wedding, devoting much of his time to warning about the wrath of Hell for those who break their vows. Jake wore a narrow black knit tie, a new short-sleeved white shirt, polyester brown pants, white socks, and Salvation Army black lace-up shoes that had been somewhat polished. He did not smile, his narrowed eyes always shifting. Rhoda wore her homemade long white organdy dress, a droopy blue bow pinned above her heart near the high lacy neckline. Her face was thin, her cheeks blushed bright red from too much makeup, but her blue eyes sparkled and the corners of her narrow mouth turned up.

The eighteen remaining class members returned to school in the fall. Cecil provided a continual stream of entertainment all year. Jack carried the basketball team to a district championship. Roy kept making straight *As* and was hell bent to join the Air Force. Billy worked the cornfields and wheatfields on the farm, went to the Methodist church, and lived and watched the slow pace of Sycamore Cove life.

On Christmas Day. Rhoda had a nine-pound baby boy. The last time Billy saw her, she was in Homer Waycaster's store with the baby balanced heavy on her hip. She was buying Lava soap, Camel cigarettes, and a copy of *True Romance*. The crying baby wore a heavy yellowed diaper. Rolls of fat hung from his arms and legs, pasty, like piles of mashed potatoes. Billy thought he saw a bruise on Rhoda's forearm as she extended it from her sleeve and reached out to sign the note Homer placed before her. Jake, in his plaid shirt, was waiting. He was leaning against a rusting, black 1950 Pontiac Chieftain with gray primer paint on the right front fender. He was resting one arm on top of the car, pumping high test gas with his other grease-stained hand, and squinting his eyes away from the smoke of a short cigarette stub clinging to his lips.

Nora Fletcher pulled back her long dark hair, twisting it into a bun. She never wore it like that except when she went to church. Usually, she piled it on top of her head and fastened it with about fifty bobby pins. But tonight, the bun would be round, tight, and secured with her decorated bone combs.

Jehue stood in front of the closet mirror knotting the only tie he owned. He'd already put on his one white shirt and his only suit, dark brown and a size too small. Four pairs of polished Sunday shoes were lined up beside the space heater.

"It's just once a year. Won't hurt you to go," Nora said.

"We go to church ever Sunday, and Preacher Henley always has altar call. Why do we have to go to a whole week of it?" Billy asked.

"When they have church, we go to church, and that's just the way it is," Jehue said. "We're supposed to."

Before pulling out a pair of bleached, sun-whitened socks, Jehue fished around in his dresser drawer, messing up the order Nora had carefully created. She had already put on her gardenia dress and was ready to go. Jehue slipped on his coffee-colored wingtips.

Jehue, Nora, Ron, and Billy trooped out to the washed and waxed '51 Chevy coupe for the one-mile trip to Sycamore Cove Methodist Church. All the Fletchers were proud of the church, built by the Methodist farmers in the valley. It had replaced the little plank church down by the school, where some circuit rider had converted the ancestors of the current generation of farmers—not stopping their noble whiskey-making heritage but certainly adding some guilt to the process. Jehue's father,

Elihue, and the other valley farmers had built the current church out of rounded rocks from the valley's river. Only two years ago Jehue had persuaded the Clinchfield Railroad's section manager to donate a bell from one of the old steam engines for the church steeple.

Unlike the congregation of Jesus of the Resurrection Free Will Baptist, the Methodists didn't whoop and holler during service. Seldom did anyone even say *Amen*. Billy's cousin Danny claimed that the Resurrection congregation stood on pews, ran around, and passed out on the floor, cold as a kraut rock. All the Baptists acted strange to the Fletchers, who usually required alcohol for their whooping and hollering. Billy's grandmother, Arabelle Westall, a quiet pious woman, went to Poplar Hill Baptist, a more restrained branch where congregational speaking was limited to a few men, who responded with *Amen* to almost everything the preacher said.

The family climbed the wide concrete steps leading to the small square entrance hall, the boys lagging behind. If they arrived at the right time, Preacher Henley let the young boys take turns pulling the chord to ring the bell for eleven o'clock service. But not today. Jack Holtzclaw had already rung it.

No greeters or ushers met the family, and no one handed out bulletins—they weren't needed. Everyone knew the songs and order of the service—the same every Sunday except Easter and Christmas. Tonight, as happened every night of revival week, Preacher Henley said his long opening prayer, which finished with the Lord's Prayer. The congregation sang one hymn, never more than three stanzas, except for "Amazing Grace," and Preacher Henley went straight into his sermon. It always started slow with a good and merciful God, revving up to an angry God who would burn all sinners in Hell if they didn't repent and be saved. Preacher Henley's voice rose and fell in pitch, intensifying into stern loud accusations that the whole congregation was responsible for being born sinful. All bowed their heads and asked for God's mercy, but did so quietly. By the time the service ended, some would proclaim they'd been born again.

Billy sat with his mom and dad in their usual place, right side, fourth row from the back, while Ron joined one of his friends across the aisle. Roy Hollifield, whose family sat at the other end of the Fletcher pew, scooted beside Billy. They whispered during the service and whiled away the time playing "between the sheets" with song titles in the hymnal. Jehue cleaned under his nails with his Barlow knife while Nora sat quietly beside him, listening but not hearing, lost in thoughts of duties yet to be done. Still, she shot Roy a stern look when he whispered, "'Open Now Thy Gates of Beauty' between the sheets!" Billy elbowed him in the side, and the boys stopped talking but continued turning pages, pointing at titles and choking back laughter until they were bored. Only then did they pay any attention to the preacher.

The sermon droned on for nearly an hour before Preacher Henley's tone rose to a climactic pitch: "And now, as we sing together, *Just as I Am, Lord, just as I am,* won't you come? Won't you give your life to Jesus? Won't you save your soul from torment? Listen for that still, quiet voice telling you to come just as you are. He'll accept you just as you are, without condition, and your life will be changed forever as you are born again in the Spirit." In a reverential softer tone, he continued, "Listen to the words of this beautiful old hymn and let Jesus flow into your heart. Let's sing together now. Miss Hettie, will you play softly as we wait for the Spirit to lift us from our seats to come, to come to the altar and accept Christ?"

Billy's great aunt Hettie Fletcher played sweetly, and everyone sang, "*Just as I am without one plea, for that thy blood was shed for me,*" broken and quiet at first, then louder as the preacher's words sank into their souls. Gilbert Johnson, an elderly farmer, had already gone straight to the altar as usual. Teary-eyed, Rhoda Bartlett, looking tired with her long stringy hair and her wrinkled housedress, also went up, leaving her fat little boy on the back pew with her none-too-happy husband, Jake.

"You want to go up?" Roy asked.

"Why?"

"Other people are going up."

"You want to go up with Rhoda Bartlett?" Billy asked.

Bertie Fletcher pushed herself up with her cane and limped to the altar as the last stanza of the hymn played. Ralph, her son, held her arm. Church regulars, they always sat in the front pew. Preacher Henley signaled Hettie to stop playing.

"The Lord is working in this congregation tonight, I feel it. He's reaching out to each and every one of you. Come now, brothers and sisters, as we sing the first stanza once again. Listen to the words and let them move you."

"Aw look, others are going, Rhoda don't matter," Roy said.

"I'll go up if you will," said Billy.

"Okay, but you gotta go first."

Billy sat through a couple more bars, then slowly stood. "Let's do it." He pulled on Roy's plaid sleeve and, side by side, the two walked slowly to the front. Billy kneeled beside Rhoda, who sobbed quietly as Preacher Henley laid his hand on her head.

The preacher moved on to the boys, whispering, "Praise Jesus," he placed his heavy hand firmly on each boy's head, lifting his other hand high as he said to the congregation, "See what the Lord has done! He has

182

brought these lambs into the fold."

Hettie switched to "Amazing Grace" as Preacher Henley coaxed others, without success, to come forward. After Hettie had played "Softly and Tenderly" twice, he gave the benediction: "And now, may the grace of our Lord and Savior Jesus Christ be with you all until we gather tomorrow night."

The preacher escorted the saved down the aisle so the congregation could bless them as they left. Most everyone, especially the older women, hugged the stiff boys and said how proud they were. Preacher Henley gathered the saved in a circle. "If you're a new convert, stay here a minute, please. I need to talk to you."

Billy loitered with Roy and Rhoda just inside the door, noting the dirty look Jake threw their way as he lit a Camel and propped himself against a column at the bottom of the steps. The baby whimpered in the arms of one of the stalwart women of the church. Billy glanced back up the aisle and saw his parents huddled with Roy's, their mothers dabbing their eyes with handkerchiefs.

Preacher Henley returned. "Now that you three have been saved, you should be baptized if you've not already been sprinkled when you were babies." None of them had.

From past experience, Billy knew baptizing wasn't much different from being saved—the preacher said some different words and stuck his hand in water, then laid it on the person's head, said more, prayed, and that was it.

But the preacher had different plans for these late-bloomers. "You can be sprinkled in the church, but, since it's summer, I want to baptize you in the river."

"I'd like to be baptized in the river," Billy said, knowing his mother's preference.

"Me, too," said Roy.

Rhoda, never looking up from the floor and still sobbing, said, "Okay."

"That's good," said Preacher Henley. "If the weather's good, we'll do it in the swimming hole down at the Iron Bridge next Sunday after the regular service."

The Iron Bridge was on Flint Station Road which cut off the main highway. Entire families used the swimming hole for cooling off in the hot summers. Some high school boys dove from the bridge. Others dared to jump from the top support beams arching over the bridge. Smaller kids watched the brave older boys with envy while those diving made sure the girls were watching before their daredevil leaps.

The following Sunday, Preacher Henley delivered a chiding sermon. Disappointed by his mediocre success during revival week, he unenthusiastically reminded the congregation about the baptism after the service. While most of the congregation left for their usual Sunday chicken dinners, a handful of the most devoted church members formed a short, funeral-like procession to drive the three miles to the bridge. The preacher led in his '54 wood-paneled Ford station wagon.

When the group arrived, they found several youngsters in the swimming hole. Preacher Henley walked onto the bridge, surveyed the site, and waved his frayed Bible, calling to those in the water to get out so that the church could have the baptizing. They all obediently did as he asked. His silver hair and confident voice went unchallenged. He returned the Bible to the station wagon and took off his tie.

The baptismal candidates lumbered down the bank to the water's edge, Preacher Henley giving young Rho-

da a steadying hand. Wading into the waist-deep shallow edge, he stirred up mud the same color as his polyester pants.

Half-naked swimmers, parents dressed in their Sunday best, and the congregation members formed an odd silhouette on the bridge against the bright sky. The choir director rallied the audience into a ragged version of "Shall We Gather at the River."

The preacher nodded for Rhoda to join him and she complied, leaving her shoes at the shore. She wore a white lace dress with a big red flower hanging below her high-buttoned collar. The gathered skirt of her dress billowed, then sank below the water. Jaw set, her hard eyes seemed focused far away. Jake, now with one black eye, stood holding the baby near the end of the bridge away from the others.

Placing his hand gently on her back, the preacher lowered her carefully under the water. In seconds she rose from the water as though levitating, her hair draping down her back like the shawl of Mary. Onlookers concentrated on her serene face, trying to avoid glances at her perfectly contoured body, now revealed by the clinging dress. Roy and Billy watched. She seemed not to notice as she stared straight at Jake. Lena McGee tossed a towel to the preacher, who wrapped it around Rhoda's shoulders as he helped her to the bank. Her red flower floated downstream and disappeared.

Roy and Billy had agreed to wear old tennis shoes and blue jeans over their swimming trunks for the occasion. When Preacher Henley motioned for him, Roy moved into the water and stood by his side. Preacher Henley pinched Roy's nose as he held his hand over his face. "I baptize you in the name of the Father, Son, and Holy

Ghost." Bracing Roy's back, he quickly dunked him. "Go now and serve the Lord," the preacher commanded as Roy surfaced and waded back to dry land.

Billy handed his glasses to Roy and sloshed forward when Preacher Henley motioned to him. Repeating the nose-hold and back brace, the preacher announced, "I baptize you in the name of the Father, Son, and Holy Ghost." But, just as Preacher Henley lowered him, Billy's feet slipped in the mud and he did a complete back flip over the preacher's arm. His feet thrashed above the water, splashing the preacher before his head surfaced. He gasped for air, coughing and sputtering river water from his nose and mouth.

Preacher Henley grabbed Billy by the collar and lifted him up like Charlie McCarthy, holding him high while snot and muddy water flowed down his disoriented face. "You okay, boy?" Without waiting for an answer, he took Billy's arm and wobbled him to the bank. "Go in peace and serve the Lord," he said, pushing the boy up the muddy slope.

The saved all on solid ground, Preacher Henley exchanged hugs with each, pronouncing them baptized. "Someday you will understand this more than you do now." Cheers from the crowd above rose as a fat boy yelled from the top girder, then cannonballed off the bridge. A tidal wave flooded around the already sodden group standing below, washing the mud from Billy's feet.

The week of revival at Sycamore Cove Methodist church was over. Billy had gotten baptized by Preacher Henley in the swimming hole down at the Iron Bridge. He was changed, born again, or so they told him. It was time to do something different or to be something different. He went to school every day, attended church on Sundays, worked and played in the fields and mountains of Sycamore Cove, had an occasional wet dream, looked at the lingerie ads in the Sears Roebuck catalog, and thought of what it might be like to have sex someday. Yet he was a sinner who was now washed clean and saved.

He knew he had been a sinner because his grandmother and Preacher Henley had told him so. His grandmother, Arabelle Westall, was a Hard Shell Baptist who put all her faith in the King James version of the Bible. She thought it was a sin to dance and tolerated no music other than gospel. Once, when a couple of Mormon bicyclists in white shirts and black ties had come to Sycamore Cove, Nora let them come in for a drink of water. They stayed two hours and talked about a couple of guys who had travelled across the country and settled down after they had seen a bunch of seagulls in the middle of the desert. Somehow that had been a sign that they should stay there and have many wives. After thanking Nora, the young men departed, leaving behind a copy of *The Book of Mormon*. Nora was in a pickle about the book. They had said it was like the Bible, and after all, it did talk about how the Mormons worshiped Jesus.

"What should I do with it?" she asked her mother, who quickly and with full authority from God said, "Burn that thang, hits the work of the devil. Don't you know that the last thing the Bible says is that you ain't supposed to add nor take away from the words?" Of course, Nora did as her mother said but couldn't help feeling guilty as she stuffed the book in the cookstove.

One hot July Sunday afternoon when Billy was a youngster, the family had treated their grandmother to a Chuck Wagon Gang gospel singing at The Oak Hill Community Center. They sat through two hours of harmony from quartets and trios, all singing a cappella versions of old favorites such as "The Old Rugged Cross," "Church in the Wildwood," "The Old Ship of Zion," and "Bringing in the Sheaves." Funeral home fans fluttered in rhythm, and several men said, "Amen," at appropriate times. Skinny tenors chimed their high harmony with melodies driven into the attendees' bones and souls by the booming bass of big, hairy men. When they had finished with "I'll Be No Stranger There," the family left.

"How did you like it, Momma?" asked Nora.

Arabelle's mouth was permanently puckered, showing no sign of lips. She was short but strong, a little bent with age, but she held her head high and mighty. Her mostly gray hair, not cut since she was saved, was pulled tightly back into a neat round bun, held in place with bone combs. She wore a well-worn, long sleeved straight dress, a size too big, with a Jesus cameo broach at the collar. The plain gray dress had no waist and covered her cotton stockinged ankles that rarely showed above her high-top, black laced shoes. Arabelle loosened the starburst of wrinkles around her mouth enough to reply, "They was a Godsend fer them that listen to all that other kind of sinful music. They was good, but if a person don't watch it, they can get caught up in even that sort of thang for the wrong reasons—I almost felt like patting my foot."

Billy never had any interest in prolonged visits to Grandmother Westall's home. Arabelle's righteousness left no room for teasing and jokes or big, elaborate meals, unlike his grandparents in the Cove.

Youth Sunday was to be held in the nearby Methodist churches a few weeks after Billy's baptism. Local churches invited any boy who "felt the call" to come to one of the church pulpits and deliver a sermon. After Roy Hollifield and a few of the older boys had volunteered, Billy joined the crowd, although he had never cared for visibility, always preferring to blend with the group. But he had gotten caught up in the spirit of the moment and had forgotten one small detail. He had agreed to preach a sermon, alone, in a pulpit, before a bunch of strangers, at their own church. But backing out would be humiliating, and even worse, he would forfeit forever any chance for gaining the respect of Amy Cox.

The social lives of the young people were deeply intertwined with the church. Every Sunday they met at different regional churches, particularly enjoying the outings near mountain landmarks and tourist attractions, where they participated in activities such as walking down the long trail to Buckeye Falls with no light at night. There, in the darkness of the dense laurel and rhododendron, the boys could hold hands with the girls, who screamed and shouted at every hoot owl and Chuck-will's-widow that called. Sometimes they would ride out to Eagle Rock Overlook to watch for the mysterious Brown Mountain Lights, which they all at least pretended to see. The group sat on the rocks there on a Saturday night a week before Billy's scheduled sermon.

"Over there!" Jack pointed. "There!" he pointed again.

"I don't see anything," said Roy.

"I see it!" said Pansy, sitting next to Jack.

Faint lights glittered along the ridge, miles beyond the little group giggling and occasionally singing "We are Climbing Jacob's Ladder" or "Twenty-Six Bottles of Beer on the Wall."

"Where are you preaching, Roy?" Billy asked.

"I got Parkview," he said.

"What are you going to preach on?"

"Jesus is like a light, beckoning us in the night," said Roy, looking across the ridges. "How about you?"

I don't know yet. I'm gettin' scared. It's next Sunday and I can't come up with nothing."

As the week passed, Billy racked his brain for ideas, trying to remember verses. Never a biblical scholar, he could recall only passages involving Christmas—wise men, Mary and Joseph on a donkey following a star, but this was August. He thought about Jonah and the whale but couldn't see the relevance. They were in the Blue Ridge Mountains, nowhere near the ocean, and the fish in Laurel Creek were trout, hornyheads, sun perch, and suckers.

After he had finished breakfast, he decided to take Jehue's old twelve-gauge up into the woods to seek inspiration. As he walked out the back door and started across the yard past the chicken house, he looked at the steep mountain ahead. Thinking back to the trip to Eagle Rock and Roy's idea about Jesus beckoning in the night, he felt his inspiration. He would use the mountain. Running back to the house, through the kitchen, and into the living room where Nora kept the family Bible lying on a hand-crocheted doily, he reached for the sacred book.

What's the big hurry?" asked Nora.

"I've got it, what I'm going to preach on tomorrow!"

"That's good," she said. "I knew you would figure it out."

Billy was not a diligent student in school or in church. He knew only the Bible verses taught in Vacation Bible

191

School. He had paid little attention to scriptural citations presented by Preacher Henley every Sunday. Flipping through the Bible, he finally figured out that the red lines were the parts Jesus had said.

Much of what he read was confusing, passages about double-edged swords, and lions and lambs and pillars of salt. He couldn't pronounce the names of people and places, and couldn't comprehend all of the *begats*. Finally, after a two-hour search, he found some verses he thought he could understand: Matthew 18:12, "…doth he not leave the ninety and nine, and goeth into the mountains, and seeketh that which is gone astray?" and Deuteronomy 34:1, "And Moses went up from the plains of Moab unto the mountain of Nebo, to the top of Pisgah, that is over against Jericho. And the LORD shewed him all the land of Gilead, unto Dan." Billy copied the verses and read them several times; he was ready.

Billy had been assigned to Beulah Methodist, near Buckeye Falls. It was a small gray-rock church formed in the days of the mountain circuit riders, a pretty church nestled among large oaks and beech trees with a western view of the ridges. Since the current pastor alternated between two churches and this was his off-Sunday, it was a perfect opportunity for some future servant of the Lord to practice preaching. The congregation was small; only twenty-five or so members attended regularly.

The day was bright, sunny, and cool. Billy drove Jehue's '51 Chevy, arriving early and sitting in the car until most of the congregation had arrived. They were all exactly on time, driving in like an orderly little funeral procession. Although Billy avoided getting out of the car, Grover Franklin spotted him and urged him to come on in.

"Hey boy, I hear you're preachin' today," he said.

"Yeah, I guess so."

"Well, I'm expecting you to save a lot of souls. God knows Dixon County could use 'em. You're gonna' light in on all the bootleggers, ain't you?"

Grover laughed at his own comment, but saving souls had never crossed Billy's mind. He smiled a little at Grover's joke and walked on into the church. Happily, he realized that he was acquainted only with Grover and a few relatives too distant to count. On his way, he could feel eyes following him to the front of the church. Many sat in their usual pews, their stern faces as set as the stone surrounding them. The few children stayed outside and played in the graveyard during the service. The women wore print dresses falling well below the knee, the collars high buttoned. The men, tieless, wore ironed plaid shirts and creased, dark pants. A few nodded politely at their silent visitor.

Suddenly, a high-pitched voice soared from a young woman leaning out of the open window: "You ain't supposed to step on the graves, Midge! Stay behind the headstones!"

Jodie Fox was standing by the piano. Her high brown hair had recently been tightly permed and was still aromatic. "We're real glad to have you with us today," she said as she sat down at the piano. Fanning her gingham skirt over the bench before sitting, she clasped her long fingers together over the keyboard.

As church superintendent, Grover had been instructed by the preacher in the proper order of the service: the opening prayer, a previously selected hymn, "Abide with Me," the Doxology, the sermon, the offering, a final hymn, and the benediction. Billy knew the order, exactly that of his own church. He relaxed with a small sigh.

Grover was a big man, fortyish, well-tanned from

field work except for the pale ring around his freckled, red-fringed bald head where his hat had shaded it. He commanded attention. The hum of gossip and curiosity fell into silence. "Let us all bow our heads in prayer," he said.

As he sat in the preacher's big walnut chair, Billy felt a chill spread over his body. The chair surrounded him, hovered like the hand of God. He could not hear the opening prayer or the hymn, but suddenly he was aware of the Doxology. His time had come.

"This here young fellow is Billy Fletcher," said Grover. "He's our youth preacher today. You all make him welcome, I know you will. Let's hear what God has put upon his heart to share with us today. Billy, the pulpit is yours." Grover sat down beside his wife on the front pew.

Carrying the family Bible with little strips of paper sticking out of it marking his verses, Billy pulled himself out of the big chair and climbed the four steps to the pulpit. It was like scaling a mountain. He moved slowly, carefully laid the Book on the podium, and opened it to the first verse. He looked down at the congregation sitting silent before him.

Every face in the congregation was his grandmother, totally devout, knowing every verse in the Bible by heart, having heard every sermon ever preached, already assured of salvation, Godly to the core. And here he was, a green toad. His throat tightened and his mouth became dry as he wrestled to get the first words out. Fortunately, he could start off by reading from the Bible, as preacher Henley always did.

"Matthew, chapter fourteen, verse twenty-three says, 'After dismissing the crowds, He went up on the mountain by Himself to pray. When evening came, He was there alone.' *He*, in this verse, is Jesus who went up on a mountain. This reminds me of how we are all climbing, climbing toward Jesus, climbing up a mountain to reach salvation. How we struggle through life to get to the pinnacle." Billy was feeling better now; his connection was made between Jesus climbing the mountain and the struggles in life.

"We live in the mountains, and we know how hard it is to climb to the top. There are roots and rocks and groundhog holes that can trip us, and catbriers that can claw us to pieces. The rhododendron is so thick you can't get through it without a chainsaw. Once again, in this next verse, we see Jesus going upon the mountain. Shouldn't we try to go there too, even if it is really hard?"

"Matthew fifteen, verse twenty-nine says, 'Moving on from there, Jesus passed along the Sea of Galilee. He went up on a mountain and sat there.' We all want to get to the top of our mountain and set there, knowing we have made it. And we don't even have to climb as far as Jesus did since we're already at about 4,000 feet up here in Dixon County."

Billy felt their piercing eyes. He had to go on, searching for a way forward. "When our task of climbing is finished we all deserve a rest, to sit there and feel good about making it to the top. And we don't have to go alone like Jesus. We're all climbing together and can all sit together on top of the mountain and tell each other what a good job we did getting to the top. I know when I go out into the woods behind my house, it seems like such a long way to the top of Bobcat Mountain. I've even tried to climb to the top, but I've not made it yet. I'm going to make it one day. My dad has been to the top of Bobcat, so I can make it, and you can too. Me and Roy Hollifield went about half way up one day."

This wasn't going anywhere. Billy tried to make the

pause seem inspired, as if waiting for his last point, whatever that was, to soak in. Better get back to the *Word*, he thought.

"Anyway, Jesus was always climbing up on mountains. Listen to these inspired lines from Matthew seventeen, verse one!" he said firmly. That sounded good, like something Preacher Henley would say.

Clearing his throat, he read, "After six days Jesus took Peter, James, and his brother John, and led them up on a high mountain by themselves."

His mouth cotton-dry, Billy searched for some grand finale. But he had already shared all of his thoughts. He had made his point about the challenge of climbing to reach the top of mountains. He had nothing left to say. He didn't know anything about what Jesus, Peter, James and John did on the mountain. He couldn't remember who Peter, James and John were. Was John Jesus's brother or James's brother? Were they disciples? He knew John was a Baptist. If he was a Baptist and Jesus was his brother, then Jesus was a Baptist. It was all too confusing. And Peter built his house on a rock. But that's all he knew. His mind raced. The moment dragged on. His face burned.

"Let us pray!" he said!"

"Our Father who art in Heaven, hallowed be thy name, thy kingdom come, what will become, forgive us Lord our daily bread and give us our trespasses that lead us beside the still water. Deliver us from evil, for thine is the kingdom, the power and the glory, I pray thee Lord our soul to keep forever and ever. Amen, Amen!"

He closed the family Bible, leaving it on the podium with the strips marking his places. He stepped down from the pulpit. Staring at the floor, he sat back in the preacher's big chair, sinking even deeper into it, so deep that he disappeared. The congregation sat silent, the time creeping by, the seconds ticking into hours. Grover Franklin finally stepped up from the front pew and started the offering plate to finish the service. Quickly he picked out the final hymn "Be Still My Soul." The congregants all sang with fervor:

> Be still my soul: The Lord is on thy side.
> Bear patiently the cross of grief or pain.
> Leave to thy God to order and provide;
> In every change, He faithful will remain.
> Be still, my soul: thy best, thy heavenly Friend
> Through thorny ways leads to a joyful end.

Billy tried to still his soul. He felt like it was tangled in a laurel hell or catbrier thicket. Every line stung him with regret and fear of the now and the hereafter.

Vernon Fox gave an unusually long benediction, especially asking God to watch over the young preacher and help him make something of himself someday. Grover reached down into the big preacher chair, found Billy, and pulled him out, leading him to the door ahead of the congregation.

Shaking Billy's hand politely, they thanked him as they smiled and chatted quietly on their way out of the church, in curiously good spirits. Billy pulled out his pocket watch; it was 11:35. He wondered what Roy Hollifield was doing. The congregation got into their cars and left as they had arrived. They had buried a preacher that day, but not in the Beulah Methodist cemetery. Billy walked across the little gravel parking lot, pitched the Bible on the back seat of the '51 Chevy, and drove slowly back down the mountain.

Holy Night

Whither goest thou, America, in thy shiny car in the night?
—Jack Kerouac

They were on their way home from the Billy Graham Crusade in Charlotte and had just passed the lime quarry at Woodleaf, about six miles from home. They'd been saved again— gone down to the coliseum floor with about a thousand others, where they were greeted by people waiting to hug them and get their names and addresses.

Viola Biddix, a bright-eyed girl with dimples and long, loosely curled brown hair, had descended first, tears streaming down her round cheeks. Viola acted shy, yet among the boys her behavior had created the impression, or perhaps the hope, that she was easy. She led Cecil Pentland, normally the class intimidator, down the bleacher steps with a tight grip. Next came Roy Hollifield, followed by Billy Fletcher, who joined in mostly because he had driven and didn't want to lose them in the crowd.

Tomorrow they would return to school where they would embellish the details of the night, this holy experience, when recounting it to the other fifteen members of the eleventh-grade class. Riding shotgun, Roy had fallen sound asleep almost immediately. Cecil and Viola rode as one in the back seat, wrapped around each other in the darkness. Billy fought to keep his eyes open, lulled by the hum of the engine and an occasional half-hearted "don't" or "stop" from Viola. Trying to stay alert, he thought about Amy Cox, his angelic blonde crush, and had the faint hope his newly cleansed soul would appeal more to her than had his old one.

An explosion suddenly shook the car, the Chevy's engine shuddering so violently it shook the tailpipe loose from the baling wire Billy had used to cinch it. The pipe scraped and bounced along the pavement, showering sparks that from the rear looked like the finale of a fireworks show. It lit the interior of the car enough for Billy to see Cecil yank his hand from under Viola's tight angora sweater.

She screamed and Cecil shouted, "What the hell was that?"

Billy veered the juddering car into the grass at the edge of the road and cut the switch. The engine rocked to a stop, and all fell silent except Viola, now gasping for breath. Billy shut off the headlights to save the nearly dead battery.

"Did somebody shoot at us?" Roy asked, now wide-awake and tangled in the maze of wires under the dashboard. "Shouldn't you all get down? They may shoot again."

"Ain't been shot unless they shot through the engine block, you numbskull. Get up off the floorboard and help Billy find out what happened," said Cecil. "Calm down, Viola, they ain't nobody shootin' at us. Something's just wrong with this damn junk pile. I knew I shoulda drove the Olds."

"You shouldn't talk like that tonight," sobbed Viola.

With no handle inside, Billy rolled down the window and reached outside to unlatch the door. Roy, back in his seat, waited until Billy had walked around the car, just in case. "Get out and help us figure out what happened, Cecil," Roy said. "You know more about cars than the rest of us." Roy didn't dare admit he and Billy knew as much as Cecil about cars. As the owner of the biggest, fastest automobile in Ferguson County, Cecil treasured his reputation as an expert. The only reason he hadn't insisted on driving his red-and-white, two-door V8 Olds coupe was that he'd wanted to make out with Viola.

Billy popped the hood and stared at the silent engine. He'd kept the rusting, pastel-blue, four-door, six-cylinder Chevy running well beyond its time, which appeared to be now. "Roy, get the flashlight from the dash pocket. Be careful, and don't open the door all the way, it'll fall off."

The full moon behind wispy clouds revealed a few pale houses with backdrops of silhouetted trees, their autumn colors subdued in the shadows. Billy thought the moon's reflection in window panes seemed like eyes watching over the farmers, factory workers, housewives, and children sleeping inside.

Roy fumbled for the flashlight, glancing at Cecil and Viola tangled in the back seat. "Cecil, get out here and help us figure out what to do. My mom and dad are gonna be worried. They thought I'd be home by midnight."

"Aw, don't get your diaper dirty. They never wake up when you come in anyway. It don't matter how late any of us get in as long as we get home before morning. They're always so damn tired they'd sleep through thunder."

"Don't cuss, Cecil," said Viola. "You got saved tonight."

"It didn't take."

"Don't you want to go to Heaven?"

He released his hold on her, kicked the back door open, and crawled out. "Yeah, yeah, but we gotta get *home* first. Gimme the light, Roy."

Cecil sauntered to the front of the car with Roy trailing behind. He aimed the light onto Billy's puzzled face. The reflection from Billy's thick glasses shone like the eyes of the bullfrogs the boys hunted. Billy grabbed the

light and stood still until the spots before his eyes faded. He shined the beam over the whole engine. Roy and Billy leaned into the car's jaws. The engine was simple—a straight-six block with plugs and wires, a coil, carburetor, generator—the usual things in a cheap car, nothing automatic.

"I don't see nothin' wrong," said Cecil. "It's gotta be somethin' loose inside the block or oil pan to make it shake like that. Maybe you throwed a rod."

"Can't be. If that was the case, it woulda stopped dead," said Billy. I seen a car in the junkyard with a rod sticking plumb through the side of the block. You ain't goin' nowhere that way. This felt more like running on about three cylinders. But I just tuned it up. Everything's new."

"We'd be home by now if this thing was a Mercury," said Roy.

"Mercury, my ass," Billy said. "Uncle Saul said all them Ford brands are made out of old beer cans, junk pots and pans. He wouldn't buy one if he had to walk to Oak Hill every day. Besides, my dad says Mercury's a Republican car. Now, a Buick, that's a *real* car, a GM, body by Fisher. If you ever see that little coach emblem attached to the rocker panel, you know it's quality." The boys echoed their familial prejudices in their automotive conversation.

They leaned in farther in unison as if waiting for a sign from God to reveal the damage. Viola pulled herself together, slipped her saddle oxfords back on, and climbed from the car. She made her way to the front, smoothing down her skirt. Pressing against Cecil, she said, "What's wrong with it?"

"It's broke," Cecil grumbled.

They pulled themselves from under the hood, leaving

it propped open. "We'd better get help from one of these houses. It's gettin' late," said Billy. "I don't care what you say, Cecil. Our folks are gonna get up a posse. They'll think we've wrecked and are layin' dead in a ditch somewhere."

"You wake some of these people up this time of night and you'll either get a load of buckshot in your running-away ass or their dogs will chew it up for you," said Cecil.

"Aw, that's a bunch of garbage," Roy said. "These people are nice, just like everybody in the cove. We're not that far away."

"That's exactly what I'm talking about," Cecil said. "You come up to my house at midnight and see what my daddy does. It's different in the daylight. Nobody never bothers anybody. Why in the world they get so mean and pissed at night beats the crap out of me. I guess they really don't want to be woke up."

"I said stop that nasty language, Cecil," Viola said.

"Coot Rankin come up to our house one night and crawled in Dad's car to sleep off a drunk," said Billy. "When Mom heard the door shut, she looked out the window and seen somebody in the car. Scared her to death. Dad grabbed the shotgun and went out to see who it was. He wound up drivin' Coot home."

Roy looked up at the blue-white moon. "I'm getting tired of standing around here. Come on, Viola. Let's see if we can figure out what's wrong with this thing. We'll make it like another crusade tonight."

Cecil said, "What the shit are you talking about? Roy, you wouldn't know a generator from a carburetor. Billy, get back in and kick it over again. Maybe it's fixed itself, or maybe I'll see something."

Billy shook his head but got back in and turned the key. The engine roared, then shook so hard the dash pocket door fell off its hinges. Roy and Viola jerked backward, and Cecil stepped to the side. "Engine starts fine," said Cecil. "It sounds like everthing is running. Just acts like a wooly booger's got a hold of it. Let's just get in and go."

"I ain't drivin' it like this. It'll shake the whole car apart!"

Viola clasped her hands behind her back and leaned in to look at the engine, and Cecil lowered the flashlight beam to her pale, smooth legs and the crinolines that rose invitingly from beneath her skirt.

"Come on, Viola. Let's start walking up the road," Cecil said. "Maybe somebody will come by and pick us up before we make it home. These two assholes can figure out what to do about the car."

Billy gave in. "Shut the hood, Viola. We'll all go, I guess, but we'll walk all the way home. Ain't nobody out here this time of night."

Viola reached up to close the hood, lifting her skirt even higher in Cecil's beam. Feeling his presence, she turned to face him. His eyes rose, drawn up by an angelic glow lighting her face above his flashlight's beam. He quickly cut off the light, but Viola's face continued to glow like an alabaster statue of the Madonna. Cecil was about to reconsider his salvation when Viola pointed. "What's that hole in the hood? The moon's shining right through it."

The boys rushed to study the perfectly oval hole near the front of the Chevy's hood. "What the hell did that?" Cecil shouted.

"I told you somebody's shooting at us," Roy said. "It's a shotgun hole. Musta hit something in the engine."

Viola gripped Cecil around the neck while Billy grabbed the flashlight. Roy ran back to the car and the floorboard, cracking his head on the dash.

Billy surveyed the engine and said, "Shotgun, my ass." Then he walked to the back of the car, wired the tailpipe back up to the bumper, rummaged through the trunk, and returned with huge plumber's pliers and a hammer. He handed the flashlight back to Cecil, then transformed into a man of purpose, hell-bent on grabbing, twisting and beating something. "Cecil, hold the light right here."

"Well I'll be damned," said Cecil.

"What?" Viola was getting antsy.

Using the hammer and pliers, Billy beat and twisted something under the hood. When the banging and car-rocking began, Roy poked his head out the window. "What are you doing? The thing's already nearly dead. You trying to finish it off?"

In a few minutes Billy had ripped something metal from the engine and thrown it into the ditch. He slammed the hood shut, cleaned his thick glasses on his shirttail, and ordered everyone back in the car. Once all were settled, he turned the switch and the engine purred to life.

"What did you do?" Roy asked.

"One of the fan blades broke off and flew through the hood. That thing is probably in orbit by now. I broke the one off the other side. Two blades'll do in cold weather. I'll put in a junkyard fan before summer."

They rode in complete silence past Laurel Creek flats, past the Iron Bridge over the dark swimming hole where Roy and Billy had been baptized, past the turn-off to Sycamore Cove School, and into the first loop of the Clinchfield Railroad.

Billy dropped Viola off first. Cecil walked her up the short steep driveway to her dark house, where they briefly disappeared into the moonless shadows. At his house, Roy hopped out before the car even came to a stop. Cecil picked up his Olds at the end of Billy's driveway and roared away, tires throwing gravel, squealing a black curvy path of rubber on the pavement and shattering the still Sycamore Cove night.

Billy eased the Chevy up the long, two-track gravel driveway to his house. No one stirred. He parked, then leaned over the steering wheel, looking up at the full moon through the windshield—cracks splintering the light into cross-like prisms. "I gotta get that fixed," he muttered. Leaving the car, he studied the oval hole in his hood, smiling as he walked into the forgiving darkness of the house.

Blaze of Glory

Cecil drove a big, red, white-topped 1956 Oldsmobile 88 four-door sedan he'd souped up with a pair of glass-pack mufflers and chrome valve covers. He kept it washed and waxed and decorated with a cartoonish naked-woman deodorizer hanging from the rearview mirror. The car had the biggest engine Olds made, and it dripped oil everywhere he parked.

Cecil was tall and meaty. Red hair topped his small head making his prominent adam's apple appear oversized, always bobbing excessively. His eyes were close together, crowding a large nose stretching downward toward his upper lip that always arched as if he were sneering. None of his upper teeth, always visible through the arch, pointed in the same direction. Cecil was older than most of his Sycamore Cove School classmates because he'd failed a couple of grades. His superior position was based on his powers of intimidation and his fast car.

Big cars with big engines were potent symbols for the young males, who often faced rather bleak futures, typically marrying local girls and ending up in one of the furniture factories or textile mills. Most would stay in school to graduate primarily because it was the center of their social lives, where they entertained themselves and made plans for nights and weekends. Those who quit school often married out of necessity, also ending the schooling of their girlfriends. Sometimes they dropped out because of their impoverished large families, disappearing into oblivion.

Even the fathers seemed to take vicarious pride during that brief period of vitality when the sons could drive their throbbing cars to the local drive-ins and cruise the main streets. The breed of cars they drove also determined their peer status. Jack drove his father's Studebaker Hawk Coupe, small but fast, different enough from all the Chevys and Fords to set him apart. Billy couldn't compete, with his high-mileage, baby-blue '54 Chevy which Jehue had helped him buy just so he could have a car of his own. He had been driving Jehue's '51 Chevy Deluxe, totally lacking in prestige, that had replaced the Jeep Panel Wagon. Roy Hollifield was in another world with his little Simca import. The others envied Roy's car only because it was an odd-looking little thing and brand new.

Cars weren't the sole determinant of pecking order in Cecil's class of eighteen. The athletes like Jack Holtzclaw and tough guys like Cecil were on top. Others, such as Roy Hollifield and Billy Fletcher, were near the bottom. Billy was a "four-eyes" and Roy a "book-worm." Billy just tried to blend with the others, but Roy didn't care one whit about status. He was smart and ambitious. None of the tough guys intimidated him. He was content with living in his world of books and planning his future while ignoring their taunts. Still, with so few students in the small school, they all hung out together in a sort of truce.

Like his big Olds, Cecil floated through life. Even though they didn't like him, the others hung around and rode with him. The car would easily hold six and would take on the steep mountain roads with only the occasional normal cough. "Aw, it's just a little water in the gas," Cecil would say. He drove like Satan, cutting the corners out of all the curves and flooring it on the straight stretches. He supported the Firestone tire company by leaving a thick coat of black rubber on the road every time he mashed the gas pedal or shifted into another gear.

Conventional morality was not a part of Cecil's limited mentality. Yet he had a perverted sense of duty. One night the three boys rode with Cecil toward Cedar Ridge, where they usually hung out at the drive-in burger joint. At other times they went to a similar establishment in Oak Hill. The mismatched four sat for hours, usually until closing time, flirting with girls in puny cars or with the curb hops, hoping for action that never happened.

Cecil drove them up the steep switchbacks of Buckeye Mountain, cut left down the desolate Three Mile Road, and came out by Joe Hoover's general store. They drove south past Bailey's Chinese Restaurant and Motel. Suddenly Cecil slammed on the brakes and spun the Olds, making a black doughnut pattern and heading back toward Bailey's.

Locally recognized for an incongruous menu of both exotic dishes and good southern cooking, the restaurant nestled against rugged cliffs overlooking the North Paw River. It was operated by an Army veteran who had been stationed in Asia and had married a Chinese woman. They moved back to Dixon County, bringing one of the earliest Chinese restaurants to the Carolina Blue Ridge. Their nicely landscaped garden was awash with flowers, mostly tulips, around the big dragon-framed roadside sign.

Turning off his headlights, Cecil cruised blindly toward the big sign. He turned off the engine, coasting down the grade to a stop on the road's shoulder. Jumping out of the car, he ran into the darkness. Silhouetted by the bright sign, his dark figure moved with purpose. A few minutes later he came back, both hands filled with bundles of tulips he could barely carry. Stems pointed glowing brilliant blooms in every direction. Roots dan-

gled, showering dirt behind him. He opened the back door, shoved the flowers—roots, dirt and all —onto Jack's lap, jumped back into his seat, and roared away, peeling another layer off his Firestones.

"What the hell is this?" asked Jack, peering through the blooms.

"It's flowers, asshole, can't you see?"

"I know it's flowers, you crazy son of a bitch. What did you steal them for?"

"I hope the crap nobody saw you. They'll have Sheriff McKinney after our asses. He knows your car like his own, not to mention the state troopers," Billy said. He had never done anything illegal in his life. He had never even had a beer, only a little of his Uncle Saul's homemade peach wine.

"They're for my mom," Cecil said.

"Your mom? Why the hell would you rip up the Baileys' flowers for your mom?" asked Jack.

"She's in the hospital," Cecil said, calmly cruising on toward Cedar Ridge with his elbow resting out of his window. "Keep them flowers out of the wind. It's too damn hot in here to roll up the windows. I'm taking my mom some flowers. She's in the hospital in Cedar Ridge with pneumonia, and she likes flowers. I want to perk her up."

"But with flowers you ripped off?" Roy said.

"Where the hell are we gonna buy flowers this time of night? You got any better idea? Besides, we've already got them now. You want me to go stick them back in the ground?"

So that night after they trimmed the tulips, they went to the hospital. Cecil and Jack bundled the flowers as neatly as they could in a newspaper Cecil picked up in the lobby. They walked the long hall to room 112, trailed by Billy and Roy. The fiftyish, gray-haired and overweight woman smiled sweetly and reached out one hand toward Cecil as he went in. The others quietly filed into the room, standing near the door.

"Cecil! I thought you weren't coming today," she said, propping up toward him on her elbow.

"You know better than that Momma. I've been here ever day, ain't I? Are you doin' any better?"

"Still coughing a lot, but they think they've got it under control. I shoulda knowed you'd be here," she said. "I guess you've been busy at school and at the orchard. Did you and Daddy get all of the spraying done?"

"Yeah, it didn't take long. We done it right when I got home from school. Hey Mom, look who I brought to see you."

The trio all nervously nodded hello. Billy didn't like hospitals anyway. He had been in one only after his brother got tonsillitis and the doctor convinced Nora and Jehue to have both brothers' tonsils removed at the same time.

"Well, honey, I'm glad to see you young fellers. You'll have to come home with Cecil sometime when I'm better. I'll make you some fried apple pies," she said. "Everbody knows I make the best pies of anybody in these mountains, use lots of real butter."

Cecil handed her the big bundle of tulips. "Maybe these'll perk you up."

"Ohh, they're beautiful! Where on earth did you get them?" she asked, grinning with her broad mouth, showing where Cecil got his crooked teeth.

Cecil stumbled around to find a quick answer. "We stole them," he said with a laugh.

"You did not," she laughed.

"You know better'n that," Cecil said. "Jack's mother

grew them. She had so many in her garden, she said I could have some."

Jack frowned at him but didn't say anything. Mrs. Pentland didn't know Jack or his mother, and their paths were not likely to cross.

Billy, Roy, and Jack stayed through the short conversation about things that needed to be done at home and the instructions given to Cecil to pass on to his dad. Cecil bent over and kissed his mom on the forehead.

"Bye Momma," he said. "I'll be back tomorrow after school."

They all filed out. Cecil followed quietly back to the car. Once he got in the Olds and fired up the big engine, he was once again transformed into his roaring, maniacal self. He drove down the curvy hospital driveway and back to the Upper Street Drive-In Grill, the one bright oasis in the dark little mining town.

Just as they had settled into their evening of casual conversation and futile flirting, Sheriff McKinney's new Crown Victoria appeared from the darkness down the street, headed their way. The boys sat still and faced forward as he swung into the parking lot beside Cecil, who was chattering with a long-legged curb hop in pink pedal pushers and a tight, pastel-blue sweater. The massive sheriff got out of his car, hoisted his belly over his belt, and ambled over. The curb hop winked at Cecil. You want anything, Sheriff McKinney?" she asked.

"Cup of coffee darling," he said. "Cecil?"

"Yessir?" Cecil replied.

"What you boys up to tonight?"

"Aw, just hanging out. Hoping to get laid."

Billy's heart pounded. He couldn't believe Cecil had said that to the law. Roy, in the far corner of the back seat, just snickered quietly. Jack looked worried.

"You got your foot on the brake pedal?" asked the sheriff.

"Yeah, why?" said Cecil.

"You got a brake light out. Better get it fixed before I see you again."

"Oh crap," said Cecil. "Thanks, I'll fix it in the morning."

Keep it between the ditches, Pentland."

"I'll try. Just don't look too hard when you see me coming."

Sheriff McKinney raised a hand, waved off the comment, and ambled back to his car as the curb hop showed up with his steaming coffee. As he gathered himself into his cruiser, she waited patiently, giving Cecil a final glance.

They left the drive-in to head down the mountain to Sycamore Cove. As they went under the Blue Ridge Parkway, Cecil said, "I'm gonna take you on tonight, Jack. And I'll beat your sorry ass by half a mile."

"What are you talking about?" asked Roy.

"You sure you want to try it tonight?" Jack said.

"Hell yes," said Cecil. "If we don't make it, we'll all go out in a blaze of glory."

"Wait a minute," said Jack. "We better not take any chances, especially with them in here with us."

"Four-eyes and the wimp. Who gives a crap?"

"Make what? No chance of what? And stop calling me a wimp," said Roy.

"We're not cow-shit in here. What are you talking about?" Billy said.

"Don't get him riled up, you two. I'm trying to save your hide and maybe mine here," Jack snapped back. "Cecil, maybe we…"

"You're pissing me off now. We're doin' it!" He had

pulled alongside the highway on a gravel lot at the top of the mountain. "Get in the back seat, Jack. I want all of the weight on the rear end," he said. Jack got out, opened the backdoor, shoved Billy to the middle, and slammed the door.

"Okay, you two, here's what's going on. Last Thursday night Jack said he could coast farther down the mountain in that junk pile of a Studebaker in neutral without touching the brakes than I could in the Olds. I said I'd take him on, and he coasted a mile and four-tenths before he got scared shitless and put on the brakes. So tonight I'm going to beat his big old butt. He may be better'n me in basketball, but I can outdrive his ass any day or night."

"I don't want to do this," Billy said.

"You want to walk home?" Cecil said. "Besides, all I want to do is beat big-man Jack's record in his little old Stud haws. It's got a big engine but it's little and light, so this should be a piece of cake."

"Don't you know anything about gravity? It makes big, heavy things go downhill faster than little, light things!" Roy said.

"Ride or walk, Roy?" asked Cecil. "And when we get to school tomorrow, Billy, I'm gonna tell everybody what a chicken-shit, little four-eyed turd you are, especially Amy Cox." Billy sank back into the seat between Jack and Roy.

All was ready. Cecil pushed in the clutch and eased into neutral. The highway down Buckeye Mountain was steep, one switchback after another. It was notorious for wrecks, especially tractor-trailers that burned out their brakes or flatland tourists who didn't know how to drive on mountain roads.

The Olds crawled slowly onto the pavement and began its descent. At first they gained speed with nothing more than a few squealing tires. The speed reached thirty, thirty-five, forty. Cecil rolled down the windows, resting his arm and driving with one hand.

The speedometer climbed slowly past fifty, and they hit a steep switchback. Cecil moved to the inside of the curve, crossing the line with no thought of what was coming around the bend.

"Cecil, you're crazy! What if you'd met a car coming around that curve?" Billy shouted.

"Aw, ain't no sane people up here this time of night."

They made it through two more switchbacks. Billy, trembling, braced all of his weight on the seat in front of him. He could feel every imperfection in the road gouging through the seat. "Put on the brakes, Cecil. You're gonna kill us!"

The car hit sixty, clinging to the road with all its weight and that of the passengers. It shuddered around Dead Man's Curve. They took another curve on the inside. At times the car floated above the asphalt. Then Cecil suddenly shoved his door wide open and held it hard against the rushing wind with his left foot.

"Oh, God help us!" Roy cried. "He's bailing out!"

But instead Cecil leaned hard and reached across the car to the passenger's side. He shoved open the other door with his right hand. His long body was stretched across the seat. His left hand was on the wheel; his right hand propped the passenger side door wide open while his left foot still held the driver's side door open.

"What the hell are you doing?" Jack yelled.

"Brakes!" he shouted. "Nobody said you can't use flaps to slow the car!"

"You idiot! Stop this shit!" yelled Jack.

"Hang on men, we're about there," said Cecil.

Billy braced against the front seat. Roy, pale, had fallen silent. The wind rushed, swirling trash and tulip dirt from the car floor, stinging the boys' eyes. Jack was blazing cuss words at Cecil when they rounded a sharp curve, the momentum and wind shoving the right door shut against Cecil's muscular arm. The car rocked, finally gliding into the level stretch of road in a high hollow. Cecil sat back up, let his door close, applied the brakes, and announced his victory.

The boys were lucky to have made it through those years, the time of big cars with powerful engines. They all wrecked their cars at one time or another. Roy rolled his Simca into a field near Beulah Methodist Church. Jack ran his Studebaker down a twenty-foot bank and through a pasture fence, but it was going so fast that he muscled it back up the bank onto the road. It never drove right after that. Billy rolled Jehue's new Chevy Bel Air, Jehue's pride and joy, into the bushes when he went to sleep behind the wheel. Jehue was not angry, just glad his boy was okay. In the end they all were okay. Roy became an Air Force pilot, Jack a reporter downstate. There was no reason to hang around the Cove. All of the cars had lost their big fins.

Cecil somehow managed to graduate from high school. On graduation day he brought every member of his class a gallon of apple cider, sugared and aged a few days, which he had stolen from his father's orchard warehouse. The next week he joined the army. From time to time they heard scattered reports of his distinguished service in Vietnam, of his fearless action under fire, and of his being discharged with a Purple Heart. He married a Vietnamese girl and brought her back to the States. They opened a restaurant somewhere in Virginia and became known for their Vietnamese fried apple pie.

Billy became a biology professor at a college down-state. Occasionally, he returned to Sycamore Cove and drove up the long road to his old homeplace. The house had burned long ago, the barn collapsed, and Jehue's little garage had been blown away in a storm. All of the loose boards had been removed. Only one of the old maples remained in the yard, leafless, dead limbs broken and drooping, no longer symmetrical. Its huge aged trunk, skin wrinkled and cracked, stood shining silver in the sun.

Epilogue

And so the generations pass into history. Billy clings to memories, reconstructing stories as he recalls them, telling tales of his own journey through the years in Sycamore Cove. Faces are dim, voices are only echoes, like the sound of Clinchfield trains. Elihue, Lillian, Jehue and Nora lie within their earth among Billy's uncles, aunts and older cousins.

Billy's spirit never really left. He still loves nature— the mountains, rivers, meadows, even the sea that he never visited in his childhood. He returns to Bobcat Mountain to swim in the bone chilling water of Wildcat Creek on hot summer days. The pale pink early spring burst of laurel blossoms and deep purple blooms of rhododendron seal his connection with the place. He sits on his screen porch, listening as the sound of katydids, crickets, and whippoorwills fills the blue-time when the stars begin to light up the sky and the moon is sinking over Buckeye Mountain. He sees the car lights creeping along the highway below and listens for the occasional coal train on the same tracks that brought fireworks to the Avery family for Christmas celebrations.

Billy's children have little interest in Sycamore Cove or the land he so loves. They never lived there, never heard the old folks tell tales, never camped beside Saul's Spring, or swam in Wildcat Branch with cousins and friends. Billy worries about the fate of his world after he is gone. But for now, he exchanges memories with the few aged cousins who are still there, and with those who moved back within the shadow of their ancestors, to be buried beneath the walnut tree near Elihue, Lillian and other kin.

No one is baptized at the Iron Bridge any more. It has been replaced by a dreary looking concrete structure downstream from an industrial waste disposal. The swampy "Flats" remains filled with still, shallow pools, cattails, alder and sycamore trees. The deep call of male bullfrogs and spring peepers can still be heard on warm spring nights.

Billy returns to the place where Jehue and Nora raised him. The scorched site of his home is no longer apparent. The place is covered with weeds, wildflowers, and saplings. The view of the mountains that was within Jehue's picture window is still sublime. Billy has an ever-present urge to keep the homesite cleared, to try to preserve a few of the flowers that Nora planted. He knows he will never live there, but his soul is forever tied to that place where he can still see his mother standing on the porch wiping her hands on her apron, telling him to be careful.

 Les M. Brown, PhD in biology, a native of the mountains of North Carolina, attended Appalachian State University and the University of Southern Mississippi. He is Professor Emeritus of Gardner-Webb University. His stories have appeared in *Appalachian Heritage, Moonshine Review,* and *Now and Then.* A poet and visual artist, his work has also appeared in journals including *Pinesong, Pine Mountain Sand and Gravel, Kakalak, Main Street Rag,* and *Still: The Journal.* A Pushcart Nominee, previous winner and finalist for the Poet Laureate Award of the NCPS, Les lives with his wife, Joyce, and their cat in Troutman, NC. His chapbooks, *Cold Forge* (2022), and *A Place Where Trees Had Names,* (2020), were published by Redhawk Publications.